THE UNROMANTIC LADY

Penelope Stratton

FAWCETT CREST • NEW YORK

A Fawcett Crest Book
Published by Ballantine Books
 Published in the United States by Ballantine Books, a division of Random House, Inc., New York, and simultaneously in Canada by Random House of Canada Limited, Toronto.

Library of Congress Catalog Card Number: 95-90724

ISBN 0-449-22386-8

Manufactured in the United States of America

First Edition: March 1996

10 9 8 7 6 5 4 3 2 1

Chapter One

"Aunt, it's scandalous!"

Lady Gracebourne sighed as she met the stormy eyes of her niece. She'd known that Diantha would take the news badly, but she hadn't expected the explosion of wrath that had greeted her. "No, dear," she tried to explain patiently, "it would have been scandalous if Charlotte *hadn't* returned to her husband."

"That's what the world will say," Diantha agreed, "but *I* say it's scandalous to force a woman to live with a man who's behaved as Farrell has, merely because a piece of paper says he's her husband."

"Not merely a piece of paper, dear," Lady Gracebourne said mildly. "There are the four children, you know. And besides," she hurried on before her masterful niece could speak, "nobody is forcing Charlotte. She *wants* to return to Farrell. In fact, she says she might never have left him if you hadn't convinced her that no woman could live with a man who'd done such a thing."

"Certainly no strong-minded woman could," Diantha asserted.

"But poor Charlotte isn't strong-minded. She's still very fond of Farrell, which I know you think shockingly weak—"

"After what he's done, I certainly do," Diantha said firmly.

Aunt and niece were seated in the morning room at Gracebourne House in London. The bright summer sun illuminating them emphasized their family likeness. Both had dark blue eyes and mobile, expressive features. There the likeness ended. Lady Gracebourne's face was mild and her eyes often looked bewildered, while Diantha's air was decisive, and her chin, while dainty, was set in firmer lines than were considered becoming in a young lady.

She was commonly called a beauty, and with some justice. Her neck was swanlike, her features fine, and her complexion silky. But none of this hid her considerable disadvantages. She was outspoken to a fault, which would have mattered less if her opinions hadn't been so outrageously advanced. But from some unknown source she'd imbibed a liberal spirit, quite unbecoming to one of her age and sex. Her intelligence was sharp, but she lacked the feminine cunning to disguise the fact, and if she hadn't been a great heiress, her aunt would have despaired of her marrying.

Diantha Halstow was twenty in that summer of 1814, a late age for a girl of her looks and expectations to remain single. But it was no small task to find her a suitable husband, for while her mother had been a lady of good family, her father was the son of a banker. His vast wealth formed her inheritance. Miss Halstow's fortune might have been thought to merit a title at least, but for the smell of the countinghouse that clung to her purse.

There were, of course, men whose obligations were sufficiently pressing to make them overlook Miss Halstow's ancestry. Lord and Lady Gracebourne guarded their niece carefully, ready to see off those who offered debts but no rank to offset them. But their strict care was unnecessary. Any man who attempted to sweep Diantha off her feet found himself confounded by two eyes filled with amusement. Miss Halstow wasn't romantically inclined. She'd even been heard to cast doubt on the very existence of lasting passion.

It was this unladylike cynicism that had caused the dispute with her aunt. Lady Gracebourne's stepdaughter, Charlotte, had that morning declared her intention of leaving her parents' home to return to her erring but repentant husband. As she would take with her four ill-disciplined offspring, whose chief enjoyment consisted of making life hideous for their elders, only Diantha objected to their going.

"I really don't know what else you think poor Charlotte should have done," Lady Gracebourne protested. "Of course, her place is with Farrell, and really she—that is, they—couldn't have remained here."

"Those boys were always well behaved with me," Diantha said, correctly interpreting this last remark.

"That's because you played cricket with them all the time," Lady Gracebourne returned with spirit. "Your uncle was most displeased with the state of the lawn, not to mention the library window."

Diantha chuckled. "He wasn't displeased to have them kept out of his way, though."

"No, dear, and I'm sure we were all grateful to you. What life would have been like if *someone* hadn't been able to control them . . ." She gave an eloquent shudder.

"In any case," Diantha went on, "it wasn't the cricket that did it. It was simply a question of being firm, which is what Charlotte never is with Farrell."

"It isn't easy to be firm with a man," Lady

Gracebourne said meekly, "especially if one loves him."

"There, I knew it! Love! Charlotte married Farrell for love, and she's been as weak as water about him ever since."

"My dear, I do beg you not to say such a thing. It's most unbecoming."

"But why? The whole of society derides love. Cousin Bertie calls it a snare for fools, and I think so, too."

Lady Gracebourne gave a little scream, though whether it was at her niece's unladylike beliefs or the reminder of her scapegrace relative, it was hard to say. "What your cousin believes and what you may say are quite different things. He is a gentleman."

"Not according to Uncle Selwyn," Diantha declared irrepressibly. "I've heard him say that Bertie could be called a great many things, but gentleman wasn't among them."

"I meant, as you very well know, that Bertie is a *man*, and his opinions are not suitable for you."

Diantha put her head on one side and spoke in a demure manner that warned her aunt something dreadful was coming. "You mean it's all right for Bertie to say that love's a fine thing with a flash filly but Lord save him from a virtuous—?"

"*Diantha,*" Lady Gracebourne shrieked. "Be silent at once, and tell me how Bertie dared to say such a thing in your hearing."

"Well, I can't do both, dear aunt." Diantha chuckled.

Lady Gracebourne gathered her shattered dignity about her. "Answer my question. How did even Bertie dare to speak such words in the hearing of a young lady?"

"He didn't know I was listening. I was passing

Uncle Selwyn's smoking room, and the door stood ajar."

"You should have departed instantly."

"I know. And I didn't. It's very shocking. What's to be done with me? But you see, I have no delicacy at all and will be on your hands forever."

"It's not a matter for levity," insisted her aunt with as much severity as her mild temper could rise to. "Here you are, twenty already, and no sign of a husband for you. Nor ever likely to be while you go around declaring that you don't believe in the tender passions."

Diantha wrinkled her brow. "At any rate, I don't believe they're desirable. They seem to bring nothing but misery. You and my uncle have the happiest marriage I've seen, yet your parents arranged the match. You'd hardly met each other before the wedding."

"That's quite true. I'm glad you realize that your elders should decide these matters for you."

Diantha's eyes twinkled, for this wasn't precisely what she'd said. She meant to pick her husband for herself as surely as the most romantic young lady who ever lived, but she would choose him according to her own principles. However, she held her tongue while her aunt continued, "But while a girl shouldn't place too high a value on romantic love, neither should she announce to the world that she doesn't believe in it. A gentleman likes to feel that his bride has a genuine preference for him."

"You mean they like us to lie," Diantha stated bluntly.

Lady Gracebourne sighed. "Yes, dear, that's exactly what they like us to do, and I despair of you if you can't learn to do it."

"But how can I when all around me I see the results of relying on passion? Charlotte and Farrell married for love. Uncle Selwyn said he'd never seen a man so besotted. But look at them twelve years later. Farrell chases after every fast female he sets eyes on."

This time Lady Gracebourne merely closed her eyes in despair at her niece's unladylike language. Besides, Diantha was right. Lord Farrell was notoriously weak-willed, and though possessed of the most tender affection for his lady, was quite unable to be faithful to her for more than a month at a time.

It was true, as Diantha claimed, that society in general often mocked love, or at least pretended to, but Lady Gracebourne was uneasily aware that her niece wasn't merely adopting a fashionable attitude. Her laughter frightened men away because it gave them a disconcerting glimpse of a bitter reality. Diantha had reason for her prejudices. Her parents had made a love match in the grand manner.

Alva Crayne and Blair Halstow had fallen madly in love at first sight, but both families had opposed the marriage. Oliver Halstow, Blair's father, wanted a great match for his only offspring, convinced that his enormous banking wealth entitled him to an earl's daughter at the least. Alva's father, the Honorable Esmond Crayne, had been only the second son of a viscount, with no hope of the title. He'd planned to climb higher up the aristocratic ladder through his two daughters, Alva and Gloria. Gloria gave him no trouble, meekly allowing herself to be married off to Lord Gracebourne, a widower eighteen years her senior. But Alva had struck a tragic attitude and insisted that she would only marry for love. In the face of united opposition from their relatives, she and Blair had eloped.

At first matters hadn't gone too badly. Oliver Halstow had washed his hands of his son, but no one took that too seriously. Esmond Crayne had relented enough to hand over his daughter's modest fortune, which Blair had promptly gambled away. Reared in luxury, he'd been unable to understand that he was now a man of limited means. With terrifying speed those limits grew narrower, until at last there was nothing left.

Nobody had believed that Oliver Halstow would persist in his rejection of his son, yet now he was deaf to all appeals. He would give Blair not one penny. In the face of poverty the grand passion soured into acrimony. To the world the Halstows presented themselves as a couple who'd sacrificed all for love. In private they bickered constantly. Their daughter, Diantha, who was five at the time, watched her parents in silence.

Alva's father received the family into his country house with bad grace. No sooner were they settled than Blair departed for London, where he lived on his wits. Occasionally he returned and there were emotional reunions in which husband and wife remembered that they were great lovers with a romantic reputation that must be preserved at all costs.

In between the infrequent meetings Alva sought what consolation she could with her daughter, which, since she wasn't maternal, was very little. She alternated between neglecting Diantha and smothering her with self-indulgent emotion. These bouts of motherly devotion would be accompanied by speeches suitable to the heroine of a grand and tragic love, cherishing the child who was the last reminder of happier days. It was unclear whether Diantha knew she'd been cast in the role of "last reminder," but she regarded her mother from eyes that were increasingly disillusioned.

When she was twelve news had come that Blair

had died in London. His death had brought about Diantha's one and only meeting with Oliver Halstow. He'd arrived without warning, looked Alva up and down, and bluntly expressed his contempt. But something in the child had taken his fancy. Perhaps it was her frank, sharp-witted speech, which so precisely echoed his own. At any rate he declared that his only grandchild should be his heir.

But he attached a condition. Alva must leave her daughter's life for good. He would give her an allowance that would enable her to live magnificently abroad, but the allowance would stop if she were to set foot in England again.

Faced with the choice of luxury abroad or dependency at home, Alva wasted no time over her decision. As Bonaparte had made the continent unsafe for English travelers, and she had no aptitude for foreign languages, she chose America. Diantha, who'd been used to hearing herself referred to as her mama's sole comfort on earth, found herself with an awesome inheritance, but without a mother.

For the next eight years Diantha lived with Lord and Lady Gracebourne, growing up with their children. Having made his will in her favor, Oliver never saw her again. A year later he was dead and she came into her vast inheritance, a fact that concerned her less than the disappearance of her pet rabbit and its subsequent rescue in the shrubbery. She seemed a contented, even happy child with a lively wit and ready laughter. It might have been Lady Gracebourne's fancy that Diantha's eyes were sometimes shadowed by melancholy when she thought no one was watching her. She alternated high spirits with pensive spells when she would hide herself and read more than was good for a female.

Two years ago news had come of Alva's death in New Orleans. Diantha had listened in bleak silence, and then crept away to be alone. She refused to talk about her mother, and if she wept, she did so when there was no one to see.

Nobody ever heard her mention her turbulent early years. It seemed as though she'd forgotten them. But she never spoke of love without a ripple of amusement.

Lady Farrell and her offspring departed the next day, and for a few hours the house was quiet. In the afternoon Mr. Bertram Foxe arrived, offering to escort Diantha and Cousin Elinor riding in Hyde Park, and they accepted with pleasure.

Bertie Foxe was thirty years old, of lean build and moderate height, and with an amiable, vacuous countenance. He had a certain charm, which he used without scruple to extend the limits of a modest fortune. He charmed his way into a thousand invitations, and seldom had to dine at his own expense. He was a charming cardplayer, just managing to win more than he lost, and at his most delightful when he pocketed his winnings, explaining that he must depart for a pressing engagement without giving his opponents a chance of revenge.

He paid his servants late, if at all, but none of them would have dreamed of leaving him. Even the lady he had in keeping accepted less than her considerable accomplishments merited because Bertie was too charming to resist. His most killing charm of all was reserved for his tailor, who'd long since abandoned hope of payment for garments supplied years earlier. He continued to provide new ones because Mr. Foxe's dandified person was a credit to his art.

The only area in which Bertie had failed was in the acquisition of an heiress, for here he had to deal with fathers and uncles, a breed notoriously resistant to charm.

He'd paid unblushing court to Diantha for the last three years, much to her merriment. Even her uncle, who would certainly have forbidden the marriage, could see that her heart was in no danger, and he permitted her to accept Bertie's escort. He was just as willing to let his daughter join them, for Elinor's fortune was too modest to tempt Bertie.

It was a merry party that set off toward Hyde Park. Bertie was mounted on a chestnut mare that he'd recently purchased and whose paces he was anxious to try. He invited his cousins' admiration and they said what was proper, but their eyes danced as they exchanged glances, for they could see that Bertie had been taken in by a showy animal.

Nonetheless, he made a splendid figure astride the mare, his hat crammed at a rakish angle on his Corinthian crop, his neckcloth tied in an Oriental, his Hessian boots gleaming effulgently. The two ladies felt themselves quite insignificant by contrast.

Miss Halstow was the more striking because her tight-fitting habit showed off her tall, elegant figure to advantage. Lady Elinor Foxe was smaller and less distinguished. She was a pretty girl with brown eyes set in a heart-shaped face, framed by dark hair. In this, her first season, she'd become more popular than her dashing cousin. Some men were intimidated by Miss Halstow, but no man feared Elinor. Her understanding was good, yet not so superior as to threaten male pride. She would never, as the needle-witted Diantha did, disconcert her admirers with some sharp and unanswerable remark. But despite their marked difference, the two cousins were deeply attached.

It was June, and normally London would have been growing thin of company as society followed the Regent to Brighton, but this year was different. Following the defeat of Napoleon in April, the sovereigns of those countries that had allied to fight him had converged on London for the victory celebrations. Among them was Czar Alexander of Russia, a tall, handsome man who'd endeared himself to the English by his affable manners. Diantha and Elinor had seen him two evenings ago at a ball.

"He went around demanding introductions to all the prettiest girls," Elinor informed Bertie as they cantered toward the park. "And he waltzed with Diantha. What do you think of that?"

Diantha glanced fondly at her gentle cousin, who'd been passed over by the Czar but wasn't the least resentful.

"Perhaps he'll be in Hyde Park today," Elinor continued eagerly. "And he'll kiss your hand and ask if you remember him. What would you do?"

"I should incur the royal displeasure by asking him how his wife was when he last saw her," Diantha said with a chuckle. "That is, if he can remember that far back. They say he hasn't seen the Czarina for eighteen months."

"True," Bertie agreed soulfully. "His Imperial Majesty is no recommendation for the state of matrimony. But do not, goddess, judge us all by his example. Some of us are capable of true devotion and unswerving constancy. Accept my hand, accept my heart—"

"Accept your debts," Diantha finished irrepressibly.

"Pooh! A fig for money! When a heart's devotion—Whoa!"

His dramatic effect was somewhat spoiled by a skittering movement from the mare, who'd been fidgeting playfully ever since they'd gotten into the street. Bertie, who was only a moderate horseman, held her with the greatest difficulty, and his cousins were both relieved that they'd reached the park.

"Make me an offer another day," Diantha told him gaily. "It doesn't suit my mood this morning."

Bertie hauled on the mare and finally brought her under control. "Fine beast, ain't she?" he demanded breathlessly.

"Where did you get her?" Diantha demanded, evading this question.

"One of Chartridge's breakdowns. Only just coming onto the market. Not generally known."

The elderly Earl Chartridge had succumbed to a heart attack two months earlier, brought on, some said, by the death in the hunting field of his only son and heir, a few weeks before. As the son had been unmarried, the title had passed to the earl's nephew, Mr. Rexford Lytham. The new earl, though known to the ton, had not been one of its more prominent figures as his interests were mainly sporting, and neither of the ladies could remember having met him.

"Probably not," Bertie said when Diantha mentioned this. "Disagreeable fellow. Devilish nasty temper. Got a lot to be in a temper about now. The old man left the estates in a mess. Chartridge is selling up to meet the debts. Shall we go a little faster?"

This question was provoked by desperation as the mare was already going faster, whether the rider would or no. The ladies urged their horses into a canter, but no sooner had the mare sensed this than she picked up speed again, and suddenly Bertie was no longer with them. "He shouldn't gallop like that in Hyde Park," Elinor said, as they watched his disappearing figure.

"I don't think he has any choice," Diantha said with a chuckle. "Let's go after him. I don't want to miss the fun."

They followed Bertie fast enough to keep him in view and were just in time to witness the moment when he came to grief. He'd completely lost control of his mount, and by the time he approached the lake, was doing little more than clinging on. It was sheer misfortune that a high-perch phaeton, drawn by two matching gray horses and driven by a very dashing lady, should appear just then.

The grays reared as the chestnut crossed their path, and in another moment they, too, had bolted. The lady screamed and tried vainly to control them. Then a black horse streaked into sight, ridden by a man in a dark blue coat. With a valiant burst of speed the black thundered past the phaeton to draw level with the grays. The rider leaned over and seized a bridle, hauling backward with all his strength.

He was powerfully built, with broad shoulders, and might have averted an accident completely if they hadn't been so near the water. But at the very last second the grays fumbled for their footing on the slippery bank. The next moment they were in the lake, pulling the black horse with them, and overturning the phaeton. The dashing lady went into the water with a shriek.

"Good God, that poor woman!" Diantha exclaimed. "We must go to her aid."

"On no account must you do so."

Diantha and Elinor looked down to see who'd

spoken, and saw a landaulet that had pulled up close to them. A woman of about thirty, dressed in the height of fashion, with a cold, arresting face, sat in it, her hand raised imperiously. She was Countess Lieven, wife of the Russian ambassador, and one of the powerful patronesses of Almack's, the club from which every young lady dreaded to be excluded.

"Should we not assist her, ma'am?" Elinor asked.

"Certainly not. She's not a proper person for you to know. Besides, she needs no assistance. She has men to help her. A creature like that always has."

By now the woman was standing up in water that only reached her waist, and directing a stream of vituperation at the hapless Bertie, who thrashed madly around. She was clearly in no danger of drowning. Nor (to judge by her language) was she much in need of the delicate ministrations of her own sex. A small crowd of gentlemen had gathered on the bank, leaning helpful arms toward her. The two girls were able to give their attention to the fascinating implications of what they'd just heard.

"Do you mean," Diantha asked, "that she's a—a—?" She was longing to say the words "high flyer," but even she hesitated to be so frank before such a powerful lady.

"She is not a proper person for you to know," repeated Countess Lieven firmly. "Please remain with me. I suppose that's your ridiculous cousin who caused all this trouble?" The countess also was not easily moved by charm.

Bertie was still floundering after the mare. Nearer the bank the man in the blue coat had seized the horses' heads and was holding them while the groom uncoupled them from the phaeton. This done, the gentleman began to lead them out of the water. The ladies watching him could see now that he was about thirty, handsome in a slightly saturnine style, with a powerful, athletic figure that was admirably displayed by the way his wet clothes clung to him.

Another figure was also on display. The woman had been hauled out of the water, and her drenched muslins hugged her voluptuous contours, leaving no doubt of one shocking fact.

"Not a stitch on underneath," Countess Lieven muttered. "Just as I supposed. Shameless hussy to be flaunting herself here."

"Surely one of the gentlemen will offer her something to cover herself," Elinor murmured, blushing.

But, either from a disinclination to ruin their coats, or for a more disgraceful reason, the rescuers on the bank seemed reluctant to do this. It was left to the gentleman in the blue coat to take it off and drape it around the lady. She gave him a dazzling smile and cried, "Thank you, dear Rex," in a clear voice that carried as far as the countess's landaulet.

The man she'd called Rex turned to witness Bertie still hopelessly chasing the mare. With an oath he plunged back into the water, captured the animal with ease, and began to haul it out.

"Wretched creature," said the countess in a voice of reluctant admiration. "If I thought he had an ounce of vanity, I'd say he planned it to show himself off."

Certainly the man made a splendid picture as he strained to pull the mare up the slippery bank. His thighs, encased in skintight riding breeches, were heavy with muscles, and the thin lawn of his shirt was soddenly transparent, revealing powerful arms and shoulders.

"You know him, ma'am?" Diantha asked.

"Of course. That's Chartridge."

"Not the new earl?" Diantha said, beginning to bubble with laughter.

"To be sure. And what's amusing you, miss?"

"Oh, do let's listen to them," Diantha begged, for Bertie had struggled out of the water, and Chartridge was favoring him with a pithy opinion of his horsemanship and his judgment. The watchers were too distant to hear everything, but the words ". . . anyone fool enough to buy that beast would be fool enough to ride it that way . . ." reached them clearly, and made Diantha and Elinor choke with mirth.

"It's one of Chartridge's own horses," Elinor told the countess.

"Impossible," she replied at once. "Chartridge is a sporting man. Don't tell me that peacocky creature ever came from his stables."

"No, from his uncle's, ma'am," Diantha said. "Lord Chartridge may never have seen it before today."

"I see. Selling up already, is he? Well, I'd heard the estates were encumbered. I didn't know it was that bad. So Chartridge sold your cousin a bad horse and didn't know it." Countess Lieven also began to laugh.

"I think he knows it now," Elinor said, for Bertie had finally managed to get a word in edgeways. As he spoke a look of chagrin crossed Chartridge's face and deepened into a scowl. But at that moment the beautiful creature wearing his coat put a hand on his arm and said plaintively, "Rex . . ."

"They seem to know each other very well," Diantha observed.

"Oh, that's all in the past," the countess said abstractedly. Then, apparently becoming aware of the company, she added sharply, "And it's no concern of yours, miss."

"No, of course not," Diantha said hastily, coloring.

The crowd by the lake had broken up. The grays were now attached to the phaeton again, and the lady, still wearing Chartridge's coat, climbed in. The earl remounted his black steed and fell in by her side. Bertie clambered back onto the mare, who stood docile, evidently feeling that she'd enjoyed herself enough for one day.

Bertie made his way over to them and saluted the countess, but she immediately repulsed him with an imperious gesture. "Don't come close to me in that state, you silly creature!" she commanded. "For heaven's sake, you two girls, get him home where no one can see him."

They made their farewells and departed. The countess sat staring after them for a moment, sunk in thought. After a while she roused herself and spoke to her coachman. "John, you have a nephew in service at Allwick House, haven't you? Have the Allwicks left London for the summer?"

"No, your ladyship. They're giving a ball in ten days."

"Of course they are. Now I remember. Excellent. Take me straight to Allwick House."

"I think you should come home with us," Elinor said to Bertie as they left the park. "Mama would have a spasm at the thought of you going through the streets like that."

He agreed to this readily, for his lodgings were some distance away, and he was horribly aware that he was attracting attention.

"Did you tell him it was one of his own horses?" Elinor asked.

"I did," Bertie said. "He didn't like it above half."

He gave an audible shiver and they quickened their pace toward Berkeley Square.

Lady Gracebourne exclaimed over the sight of her husband's scapegrace nephew, but was too kindhearted to give him a scold before he was warm and dry. But when he'd been taken away to be cared for, she demanded an explanation from Diantha and Elinor, who gave it between peals of laughter.

"And it was Chartridge himself?" she asked, suitably awed when they came to the point of the story. "I'd no idea he'd returned to England. He went abroad when his brother was wounded."

"You know him, Aunt?" Diantha asked carelessly.

"We've never met, but I know of him because he's a connection of Lady Allwick. Tell me about him, my love. What does he look like?"

"He was some distance away. I formed no impression of his looks," Diantha declared in an indifferent voice.

"Oh, Diantha, how can you say that when he was so handsome?" protested Elinor. "Mama, if you could have seen the way he went to the rescue. Just like a storybook hero."

"No such thing," Diantha protested, indignant at this slander. "He behaved like a thoroughly sensible man."

She turned her head to look out the window as soon as she'd said this, so she missed the look that Lady Gracebourne exchanged with her daughter. They were sufficiently acquainted with Diantha's nature to recognize that she'd uttered a compliment of no mean order. In fact, her ladyship was able, ten minutes later, to seek out her husband and say with perfect sincerity, "My love, I believe I've discovered the perfect husband for Diantha. She saw Lord Chartridge this morning, and she's positively in *transports*."

* * *

The festivities continued unabated, but for one man in London there was little cause for celebration. Rexford Lytham, seventh Lord Chartridge, was the unwilling possessor of an inheritance that threatened to ruin him. The Chartridge estates were heavily encumbered. His own fortune, which had been sufficient for a life of bachelor comfort, was inadequate to meet these new claims. Only the sale of Chartridge Abbey, the family seat, would do that, and his pride revolted at the thought.

The one bright spot that summer was the return of his younger brother, George, from the continent. Since George had joined the army ten years ago, aged fifteen, they'd seen little of each other. But their affection was strong, if unspoken, and when George had been severely wounded in Wellington's assault on Toulouse in April, Rex had hurried to the continent. He'd planned to stay until George was fit to travel, but his uncle's untimely death had forced him to return early, alone.

George followed in June and made his way to Chartridge House, where he blinked to see his brother installed. "Dashed if you don't look strange in this stuffy place," he said frankly.

"Dashed if I don't feel strange," said the new earl. "I'd rather have stayed in my lodgings, but my man of business thinks I should 'make a presence' here to impress my creditors. I doubt if they're deceived, especially as I've started to sell off my uncle's horses. But never mind that. Let me look at you. Thank God you're looking better than when I last saw you."

That had been in a makeshift military hospital six weeks earlier. Then, George's sturdy body had been wasted with pain and illness. His thick fair hair had hung lank, and the fresh color had gone from his youthful face. Now he seemed like his old self, and his blunt features were full of life.

There was almost no resemblance between the brothers. George was of medium height and stocky build. Rex was over six foot with broad shoulders and a lean, muscular torso that tapered to narrow hips and a flat stomach.

George dressed with military neatness. Rex's clothes had an elegant perfection that might have suggested the dandy if his sporting abilities hadn't been so well known. His shirt points were fashionably, but not absurdly, high, and his cravat was tied in an exquisite arrangement. But beneath the coat of blue superfine cloth and biscuit-colored pantaloons, his figure was powerfully athletic.

The boyishness hadn't left George's face. He was fair and blue-eyed, with the air of a boisterous puppy that weeks of suffering had done little to repress. The earl was dark with a lean, handsome face that accurately reflected his thirty years. Its most common expression was one of reserve. His mouth was resolute almost to the point of hardness, and its smile was too often tinged with cynicism.

On his rare leaves home George had watched with fascinated envy as his brother attracted female attention without effort. Rex's manner toward ladies was always impeccably courteous, but his heart remained whole. Only once could George recall seeing him thaw into love, and that had been a bad business. He'd been abroad with his regiment when it ended, and Rex's letters had revealed little. When they next met, George had been awed by the air of chill that his brother wore like armor, and his eager questions had died, unasked.

His own attitude to ladies was one of humble deference. He fell in love easily and would give his devotion to almost any girl who was kind to him. This led to his being constantly in a state of infatuation, for he inspired much kindness in young women. They confided their secrets and allowed him to run their errands, but none of them fell in love with him. More than one had offered to be a sister to him.

He was sure no girl had ever offered to be a sister to Rex. That armor of indifference was a challenge to female hearts. But with George, the one person in the world for whom he had an unstinting affection, the earl's face showed only warmth.

"Frane will show you to your room," he said. "I hope you can manage to be comfortable in this mausoleum."

"I can be comfortable anywhere," George assured him. "You seem to forget how I've spent the last few years."

"I've not forgotten. I merely think that an army bivouac is poor preparation for the horrors of Chartridge House. You'll soon be wishing yourself back on a comfortable campaign. Unfortunately, not knowing that you would arrive today, I've engaged myself to dine out. But you'll have Delaney for company."

Delaney Vaughan was a relative of the earl's. He had birth, breeding, and brains, but no money. Rex, who'd always liked him, now employed him as an unofficial secretary.

"Delaney has been going over details with Longford this afternoon," he said, referring to his man of business. "I charged him to examine the figures once more to see if there's any hope."

"Just how bad is it?" George asked sympathetically.

"It seems to be a question of whether I'm faced with stark ruin or merely ruin." The earl's voice was totally expressionless as he said this, and his face betrayed nothing but boredom. George, who knew his brother's ways, gripped his shoulder for a moment.

"It's damned unfair," he burst out. "None of this is your fault. Why should you have to pay my uncle's debts?"

"The obligation doesn't fall on me, but on the estate," Rex explained. "The problem would be solved if I sold everything."

"And would you do that? Sell everything? Including the Abbey?"

"I must confess to a certain distaste for the idea. However unwelcome my inheritance may be, I suppose I have family obligations. But these are dull matters. Let's forget them until Delaney arrives. When you're settled come to my room. I must begin to dress for dinner."

An hour later George made his way along to the bedroom always occupied by the master of the house. He pulled a face at the sight of the great room with its four-poster bed hung with curtains of dark, faded brocade. "I entirely sympathize," Chartridge said from his seat by the mirror, where he was engaged in tying his cravat. Cranning, his valet, stood by with a pile of gleaming white cravats over his arm. Several crumpled specimens lay on the floor, showing that the earl had devoted much thought and effort to the task. "It's a shocking place," he went on. "Full of must and mold."

Before George could reply there was a knock on the door and Delaney entered. He was a thin, dark-haired young man in his late twenties. His clothes were well cut but sober, and his manner was earnest. His eyes lit up at the sight of George, and while the two were greeting each other the earl quietly dismissed his valet.

"Tell me the worst," he insisted when they were alone. "Can anything be done?"

"Nothing," Delaney said bluntly. "It's as bad as your worst fears."

Rex studied his cravat in the mirror and made a small grimace of dissatisfaction. "Quite ruined?" he asked in a bored tone.

"Everything is mortgaged to the hilt. Your own fortune would be quite inadequate to cover the debts."

"How very distressing."

"I could always sell out," George offered.

"That's good of you, George," Chartridge said with a warm smile. "But I'm afraid it wouldn't save Chartridge Abbey."

"There's only one thing that'll save the Abbey," Delaney declared. "And that's an heiress. The richest one you can find."

"I wondered how long it would be before that vulgar suggestion was made to me," his lordship mused. "No, I thank you."

"Nothing vulgar about it," Delaney said, stung. "Done all the time."

"Yes, by men who are brass faced enough to tell a woman frankly that they're marrying her only for her money, or hypocritical enough to pretend to tender passions they don't feel. Into which category would you suggest I attempt to squeeze?"

"Well—"

"The thought of doing either disgusts me, you know."

"You might become fond of the gel. Might even fall in love with her," Delaney suggested in a burst of inspiration. He rushed on, blithely unaware of the urgent gesture that George was making for him to be silent. "No knowing what might happen. I mean, just because you once—that is, they're not all like—" George's frantic signals had finally gotten through to Delaney, and he fell into confused silence.

Chartridge never moved, but in the mirror his eyes met Delaney's and he said softly, "Just so."

"I know what it is," Delaney said, recovering. "You're afraid she'll fall in love with you."

The earl winced. "You make me sound like an intolerable coxcomb, Delaney. I hope I'm not as bad as that. It's merely that I can't seem to meet a respectable female that I can imagine *wanting* to attach. I dislike both swooning and inane conversation."

"I know just the girl for you," Delaney insisted. "Rich as Croesus and won't fall in love with you either."

"They all do," George said simply. "No matter what he does to put 'em off, they all do."

"Well, this one won't," Delaney declared. "She don't approve of love. What's more, she don't believe in it."

"I'll forbear to point out the inconsistency of disapproving of something that one believes does not exist," his lordship said mildly.

"I mean she thinks love is all a hum; nothing but an illusion to trap fools."

"She is correct," the earl murmured, inspecting an infinitesimal speck on his frilled cuff.

"You don't mean she actually talks like that," George demanded, scandalized.

"Truth. I've heard her. She's devoted to Reason. Says so."

"Sounds like a harpy to me," George said frankly.

"She sounds like a highly intelligent young lady," his brother corrected him.

"But who wants to marry a highly intelligent

young lady?" George asked, appalled. "Good grief! She might—"

"She might prove more intelligent than oneself," the earl finished for him, amused. "That's certainly something to be avoided at all costs. You'd best marry a ninnyhammer, George. Then you'll be totally safe."

His best friends wouldn't have called George sharp-witted, but the import of this brotherly speech wasn't lost on him and he began to expostulate. "No, I say, Rex—really—I mean—" Further inspiration failed him.

"Quite," Chartridge said, grinning at him in the mirror. "Marry a ninny, dear boy. Or an heiress."

"No point in *him* marrying the heiress," Delaney explained patiently. "You're the earl, not him. It's your job to marry money and save Chartridge Abbey."

"That's right," George agreed hastily. "Head of the house, you know. Responsibilities of rank and all that."

"I'm strongly tempted to teach you a lesson by blowing my brains out, you young pup!" said his brother severely. "Then the title and its responsibilities would devolve on you. We'd see what sort of a hand you made of it."

"But you wouldn't see," George pointed out. "Not if you were dead. I mean, it stands to reason—"

His lordship closed his eyes in weary patience. "Very well," he said at last. "It was a mistaken suggestion, and I deeply regret making it. We seem to be at a standstill."

"You know how your tenants feel," Delaney persisted. "To a man they're hoping you'll marry an heiress. If the place is sold up, they'll find themselves with a strange landlord, and Lord knows what he'll be like. You might think of that."

"Thank you, I don't need instructing in how to behave to my own tenants," Rex snapped in sudden anger. "Nor do I appreciate you discussing my private business with them."

In the tense silence that followed it was George who found the courage to say, "But it ain't only your private business, Rex. They're counting on you to save them from the devil they don't know. Some of them are old friends. Corbey, who taught us to ride and—"

"Yes, I know," Rex interrupted him. "I haven't forgotten my duty, I promise you."

"Dash it all, Rex, see reason," Delaney pleaded. "This girl wouldn't interfere with your pleasures or expect you to be dancing attendance on her all the time. You'd have everything a man could ask for."

"Except a wife who loved me, it seems," the earl murmured.

"You said you didn't want that—"

"I said I didn't want a female who'd expect me to talk nonsense with her. I never said—however, it's no matter."

"You've got to marry money, Rex," Delaney said flatly. "There's no two ways about it. And better a woman you can be honest with."

"There is that," Chartridge said, still in the same languid murmur. "How do you come to know the lady's opinions, Delaney?"

"I met her in the hunting field in February," Delaney said. "We talked about a mutual acquaintance who'd recently married for love, and she expressed her deepest sympathy for both parties."

"She sounds an unusual young lady, to say the least," the earl conceded.

"Perhaps she isn't a *young* lady," George said darkly. "She's probably forty and bracket faced."

"She's twenty and completely delightful," Delaney said at once.

"Then I'm at a loss to know why some fellow hasn't secured this paragon and her wealth, whatever her prejudices may be," his lordship declared cynically. "Or is there something you have yet to tell me? Does her fortune smell of the shop?"

"It's not as bad as that," Delaney said quickly. "Actually she's a niece of Lady Gracebourne. But her grandfather was a banker."

"And?" the earl persisted, for Delaney's tone clearly showed that there was more to follow.

"Well, there's a certain amount of bad blood on that side of the family," Delaney admitted reluctantly. "Her father was Blair Halstow."

"Blair Halstow!" The earl sounded completely thunderstruck.

"Yes, did you know him?" Delaney asked. "He didn't move in the first circles, but he kicked up a bit of a dust a few years back, and of course, the way he died—"

"Delaney, let me understand you," the earl interrupted. "You're seriously suggesting that—that *I*—should marry the daughter of Blair Halstow?"

"Well, he'll hardly trouble you since he's dead," Delaney observed with asperity. "And Miss Halstow—"

He stopped and exchanged a nervous glance with George. Lord Chartridge had begun to laugh, but there was no amusement in the sound. While the other two stared at him he regarded his own reflection bitterly in the mirror, and laughed and laughed and laughed.

Chapter Two

Diantha gasped as her maid poured water over her naked body and into the hip bath, washing away the suds. They were in front of the fire in Diantha's bedroom, beginning the preparations for the long evening ahead. The occasion was a ball to mark the betrothal of the Honorable Vernon Caide, eldest son of Viscount Allwick. Having deluged her mistress, Tabitha, the elderly maid shook out a huge white towel.

But the next moment the door was flung open and Elinor bounced into the room in a manner quite unlike her usual self. She wore a dressing gown, her hair was in curlers, and she was clearly bursting with news. "Diantha, you'll never believe what—" She checked herself, and her eyes met those of the maid. "Tabs, you know, don't you?" she demanded indignantly. "You know all about it."

"I'm sure I couldn't say, miss," Tabitha said severely. "I'm not one to talk."

"You mean you haven't even told Diantha?"

"Nobody has told me anything," Diantha said with spirit. "Will one of you please share the secret?" She mopped her face with a corner of the towel.

"It's about Lord Chartridge," Elinor declared.

Diantha buried her face in the towel, concealing how the wanton color came and went in her cheeks.

"Is that all?" she asked as she emerged. To underline her indifference she gave a slight yawn.

"All? Diantha—oh, can't you imagine?"

"Not at all," Diantha asserted, rising to her feet in the bath and standing there, a young Venus in all her glory.

"My mother and father are arranging a marriage between you and Lord Chartridge," Elinor said with an air of triumph. "What do you think of that?"

Suddenly Diantha was intensely aware of her own nakedness. Heat seemed to be scurrying through her body, chasing itself in waves, each one more intense than the last. She had the alarming feeling that not only her body but also her soul was on display. She almost snatched the towel from Tabitha and wrapped it securely around her.

"I think nothing of it," she said when she could trust her voice. "It's nonsense, Elinor. You shouldn't spread such stories."

"But it's true," Elinor insisted. "Don't you recall that we were originally invited only to the ball tonight? The dinner beforehand was only for family members. But a few days ago Lady Allwick called here to invite us all to the dinner as well. It seems that Countess Lieven called on *her* as soon as she'd left us that day in Hyde Park."

Diantha raised her eyebrows. "My aunt told you all this, and not me?"

"I didn't hear it from Mama, but from my maid," Elinor said, with an air of explaining the obvious. "And she had it from Cook, whose second cousin is married to the Allwicks' butler. Everybody at Allwick House knows that Lord Chartridge is coming to the ball tonight so that you and he may meet in company and—" Elinor faltered because the look in Diantha's eyes was alarming "—and see how you look to each other. That is—you've already seen him, but—"

"But he must have his chance to look me over and see if I come up to his standard?" Diantha said in an ominously calm voice. "So this is the talk of the servants' hall? Did you know of it, Tabs?"

"Certainly, miss." Tabitha was unmoved by the look that had alarmed Elinor. She'd been with Diantha for fifteen years and knew how to weather squalls.

"And you didn't tell me?"

"I didn't wish to upset you, miss. Not with you being in such a strange mood."

"My mood is perfect," Diantha snapped.

"How can you say so?" Elinor asked. "Ever since that day in Hyde Park you've been up and down—in alt one minute and cast into gloom the next. Admit it, you did like him."

But by now Diantha had herself in hand and was able to smile mischievously and say, "On the contrary, I can barely recall him. You'd better point him out to me tonight so that I don't throw out lures to the wrong man."

"Shall you throw out lures to him?" Elinor asked curiously.

"You know me better than anyone else," Diantha said lightly. "What do you think I'll do?"

"Probably subject the poor man to a lecture on the folly of love," Elinor retorted with spirit.

"No, why should I? He isn't approaching me for love, but because his estates are encumbered."

"Oh, but you're not to be thinking that he's a fortune hunter," Elinor said.

"Am I not?" Diantha asked enigmatically.

"No such thing. He's too proud for that. Apparently he's been trying to make some sort of arrangement with the bank and shying off from meeting heiresses."

"And yet we're to be honored with his company tonight?" Diantha observed wryly.

"Only because he's fond of Vernon and couldn't get out of it. Otherwise he'd have cried off from this as well. Oh—" Elinor's hand flew to her mouth as she realized that her tongue had run away with her.

"Cried off on my account?" Diantha asked. Her voice was composed, but her eyes sparkled with indignation.

"Oh no, of course not." Elinor hurried to make amends for her tactlessness. "On account of all heiresses—because people keep pushing them in his direction, you know—and he doesn't like it. In fact they say that if it weren't for Vernon, nothing would prevail on him to—oh dear!"

She was saved from further embarrassment by the arrival of Lidden, Lady Gracebourne's dresser, who'd been instructed to oversee Diantha's preparations. She took over from Tabitha, waiting until the maid had dragged the bath from the room before she began her ministrations. Elinor scurried away to her own room to finish dressing, leaving Diantha to brood as she sat before the dressing room mirror while Lidden braided her hair.

She'd always known this day must come. A young woman's business in life was to marry suitably, and doubly so if she was an heiress. But now that things were happening she felt as if an earthquake had shaken the ground beneath her feet. What alarmed her most was that the feeling was irrational. She'd seen Chartridge and found nothing to disgust her. Now she was being urged toward a reasonable alliance with a man who was suitable in all respects. What heiress could ask for more?

But these logical arguments were chased away by the memory of a man in sodden, skintight breeches, his muscles straining as he brought the horses under control. She thought of the power that must live in that hard, athletic body, and a slow, heated sigh broke from her.

"I do hope you're not becoming feverish, miss," Lidden said. "I've never seen you with such a high color."

"Of course I'm not feverish," Diantha said quickly. "My color is due to excitement at the prospect of a ball. Don't tug my hair so, Lidden."

"I didn't think I had, miss."

"I wonder what jewelry I should wear tonight."

"Her ladyship suggested the single-strand diamond necklace and diamond pendants in your ears."

"And a bracelet?"

"Nothing else, miss."

This was an exceedingly modest array, but paradoxically it had the effect of confirming everything Elinor had said. Lady Gracebourne was far too astute to let it be gossiped that Diantha was puffing off her vast wealth. Besides, it would have been needless for her to do so.

By the time Diantha's preparations were complete she was fully in command of herself again, and able to wonder at her own brief agitation. That she, a devotee of Reason, should allow her mind to be overset by a turbulence of her senses was strange and disconcerting, but from now on she would be on her guard.

As she was surveying herself in the long mirror Elinor appeared, dressed for the ball. "You look lovely," she sighed when she saw her cousin. "Lord Chartridge will fall in love with you at first sight."

"I hope he'll do nothing so irrational," Diantha

said calmly. "I didn't fall in love with him at first sight."

"That doesn't count," Elinor maintained. "You only saw him from a distance."

"Well, I shan't fall in love with him tonight, anyway."

"Oh, Diantha, how can you talk like that? It would be delightful."

"No, would it?" Diantha asked, her eyes twinkling. "You must tell me what it's like to fall in love at first sight. I'm sure no one has done it more often than you."

Elinor chuckled good-naturedly. Her disposition was shy but affectionate, and her tender heart had led her to fancy herself in love with several gentlemen in quick succession.

Tonight she was arrayed in a delicate primrose muslin that brought out the warmth of her creamy skin, against which her mother's pearls glowed. But Diantha was glorious in a three-quarter dress of silver gauze over a petticoat of white satin. The hem bore no frills or flounces, and the long, clean lines admirably suited her tall figure. The discreet restraint of the diamonds added to her air of elegance. Lidden settled a swansdown tippet in place on her shoulders, handed her an ivory-*brisé* fan, and she was ready to depart.

It was still light when they arrived at Allwick House a little before eight o'clock, but the building was already blazing with illumination. Diantha greeted her hosts in the proper form and passed on to congratulate Vernon Caide on his betrothal. She was introduced to Marcella Bruce, a very pretty, nervous young woman who clung to her fiancé's arm.

While Diantha was uttering the polite words necessary to the occasion there was some movement in the doorway. A footman announced, "The Earl of Chartridge and Major George Lytham." Several people blocked Diantha's view. Then the crowd shifted, revealing two men who'd just entered.

One was in his mid-twenties, and his magnificent blue and silver dress uniform proclaimed a major of Light Dragoons. He had a blunt, good-natured face, topped by thick fair hair. To Elinor's entranced eyes he was by far the more splendid of the two. Diantha barely noticed him.

Her eyes were fixed on the other man, who stood surveying his surroundings with a cool gaze. He was tall and darkly handsome, with rather hard eyes. His black satin knee breeches, white waistcoat, and nicely judged cravat were unobtrusively elegant, but there was something about the man that made watchers forget the clothes. The breadth of his shoulders, the power in his long, straight legs, hinted at other, less sedate surroundings. Diantha had a sudden sensation that everything in the room had paled. Everything but him.

Lady Allwick advanced toward her new guests, her hands outstretched in welcome, and Diantha just heard the words "Rex—George dear, how good to have you home again."

Lord Chartridge greeted his hostess with a smile. Diantha, watching the civil stretching of the mouth, remembered another smile, intimate and full of shared secrets, that he'd given to the half-naked woman in the park.

The new earl was slightly known to Lord Gracebourne but not to his family. He bowed courteously as the introductions were made, and not by the flicker of an eyelid did he betray that he'd heard Miss Halstow's name. Diantha, her countenance equally unrevealing, hadn't expected him to.

No trouble had been spared to make the occasion

splendid. Over forty people sat down to dinner at a table gorgeous with silver, crystal, and shining white napery. Arrangements of pink and white roses had been placed down the center, and these were echoed by the banks of flowers in every corner of the room. Behind the two rows of chairs stood liveried footmen, their wigs gleaming white.

Diantha found herself seated opposite Lord Chartridge. She showed no awareness of him, conversing diligently with the gentlemen on each side of her. No one could have told from her demeanor that she was fighting not to look across the table. To be caught out in an unwary glance would never do, but the temptation to steal a glance at the man who might become her husband was intense.

A little further down the table Elinor was sitting beside George Lytham, talking to him earnestly. She seemed to have forgotten that it was also her duty to converse with the gentleman on her other side. Her attention was all for Major Lytham, and he, too, Diantha thought, amused, seemed oblivious of other guests. She smiled as she recognized the start of yet another of Elinor's undying attachments.

Suddenly she became aware of a pair of cool, gray eyes fixed on her. While she'd been watching Elinor, Lord Chartridge had been watching her. Now she met his gaze with a steady one of her own. He, too, regarded the absorbed couple, then looked directly at Miss Halstow. His lips twitched and a message of silent amusement passed between them. It softened his features, and for a moment his eyes gleamed with something that might have been warmth. Then the lady on his right claimed his attention and the moment passed.

The ball was to start at ten o'clock. As soon as dinner was over the party began to make its way downstairs to the great ballroom at the back of the house. Lord Chartridge took this opportunity to approach Miss Halstow and ask her to stand up with him for the second country dance. With a composed civility that matched his own she accepted. He bowed and left her.

Four hundred guests had been invited to the ball. Within a few minutes of their arrival Diantha's hand had been bespoken for almost every dance. When only one waltz remained she found George Lytham hovering bashfully by her elbow. When he begged the favor of a dance she scribbled his name in the last space. Blushing, he thanked her and retreated to the safety of Elinor's side.

Lady Gracebourne looked over her niece's card. "Nothing left," she said with a little frown. "I must own, my love, that I think you were unwise not to leave one waltz free in case—just in case."

Diantha's chin went up and she met her aunt's eyes with a look of sparkling indignation. "I'll not wait on any man's pleasure, Aunt," she said softly.

From which a dismayed Lady Gracebourne realized that Diantha knew a great deal more than she was supposed to.

The great ballroom of Allwick House was decked with flowers conveyed specially from the Allwick estates that morning. The two crystal chandeliers had been cleaned and spread a lustrous glow that was taken up by the gilt mirrors lining one long wall, reflecting glittering figures back and forth.

When the sets began to form for the second country dance Lord Chartridge approached Miss Halstow and said, "My dance, I think, ma'am."

They danced in silence for the first few minutes. But then the earl said coolly, "You must allow me to congratulate you on your fortitude in enduring the gathering, Miss Halstow. Of all things, it must be what you most dislike."

"I don't understand you, sir," she said in astonishment. "I have no aversion to dancing."

"Not to dancing, no. But surely the cause of this ball must offend every rational feeling. Vernon and his betrothed are so plainly in love, are they not? And I understand that you're no friend to this state."

Diantha was sufficiently amazed to stare at him in what she instantly realized was a most improper manner. The earl smiled as he continued, "There's no witchcraft in it, I assure you. I learned of your sentiments from my cousin, Delaney Vaughan. You met him in the hunting field a few months back and apparently expressed yourself on the subject with some feeling."

"I remember Mr. Vaughan," she said, her face lightening. "He was riding a dashing black hunter that made me pea green with envy. How fortunate he is to possess such an animal."

"He doesn't possess her. Sara belongs to me."

"To you? No, I can't believe it. You're funning."

"Why should you think so?"

Diantha chuckled. "Because I know your taste in horseflesh and I can't admire it. You like showy beasts, all sparkle and no staying power."

To one who was known as a nonpareil for his sporting ability, this remark came like a thunderclap. *"I—?"* Chartridge almost missed his footing in the dance, but recovered himself. "May I ask what I can have done to merit that?" he asked in a controlled voice.

"You sold my cousin a chestnut mare. A very pretty animal, I'll allow, but definitely bishoped."

She said these last words calmly, but with some trepidation. A bishoped horse was one that had been interfered with to disguise its true age, and such an accusation wasn't lightly made. But she had her revenge for the earl's slighting behavior in the look of sheer outrage that crossed his face. Lady Gracebourne, watching them intently, saw that look and her heart sank.

"Miss Halstow," said the earl with dangerous calm, "do you know what would happen to a man who said that to me?"

"No, and how should it interest me? I'm not a man."

The movement of the dance separated them and Chartridge was able to observe the graceful swaying of her figure at a distance. Some of the anger went out of his eyes. "Indeed you're not," he said when they met again. "You're sufficiently one of your sex to presume on it. But let me inform you that if your cousin told you that I bishop my animals, he's no judge of horseflesh."

"Of course he isn't," she concurred heartily. "Otherwise he'd never have bought that ridiculous beast of yours."

His eyes narrowed. "Is your cousin Mr. Bertram Foxe?"

"He is. I see you recall him, and the—er—encounter that you had in Hyde Park."

There was a silence. To Diantha's enjoyment, the earl's face was full of chagrin. "I'm not likely to forget," he said at last. "The mare had come from my late uncle's stables, and I'd never seen her before that day." He looked at her curiously. "I'm surprised that he told you of the incident in the park."

"He didn't. I saw it. My cousin Elinor—the lady dancing with your brother—she and I were with Bertie until he lost control of his mount and galloped off. We followed and arrived just in time to see what happened."

Lord Chartridge ground his teeth. "And did your cousin tell you, ma'am, that next day I bought the mare back from him for the same price he paid?"

"No," Diantha admitted in some surprise.

"I didn't make the original sale personally. I ordered the horses disposed of without seeing them. When I learned the truth I hastened to put matters right. It isn't my practice to gull greenhorns."

Light-footed and graceful, she swung away from him in the dance. A slight frown creased the earl's brow and he performed his steps mechanically. Miss Halstow hadn't followed the lead he'd offered her in the mention of Delaney Vaughan. In his experience, not one woman in a million could resist the discovery that someone had been talking about her. He'd expected eager pleas to have Delaney's words repeated, but she'd hardly seemed to hear. Instead, the chit had had the temerity to taunt him with an incident that filled him with mortification.

The dance returned her to him, and he took her hand as they began the final movements. "You haven't answered me, Miss Halstow," he said. "According to my cousin, you expressed great pity for a couple that had recently been so foolish as to marry for love. Did he report you correctly?"

"He seems to have done. Those are certainly my sentiments."

"Unusual sentiments for a young lady."

"But my life has sometimes been unusual for a young lady," she replied. He thought a faint shadow crossed her face, but it was instantly dispelled by laughter. "It's turned me into an awkward creature. My poor aunt despairs of me. I have many ideas that are improper in a young lady, and not enough cleverness to keep them to myself. A hopeless case."

He laughed aloud at her droll air. "Shocking," he

agreed. "But in my experience the ideas that are proper for gently bred young ladies are always dull and frequently mistaken. You do well to pursue your own line. You won't frighten away a man of sense."

"If such a creature exists," she said demurely.

"Come, Miss Halstow, you're too hard on my sex. We're not all like your cousin." She laughed aloud and he joined her. "I should like to hear some of your improper ideas," he said.

"Unfortunately the dance is ending."

"Then I shall engage you for the next one," he declared with a cool assurance that she found annoying. "Shall I get you an ice, and we can sit out and talk in comfort?"

"You're very good, sir, but I'm already engaged for the next dance, to Mr. Vernon Caide."

"Very well, the one after," he said with a touch of impatience.

The music finished. Frowning a little, Diantha consulted her card. "Not that one either," she said with a pretty air of regret. "I'm afraid I have nothing left."

Lord Chartridge ran his eyes down her card. "Why, you're quite correct. It seems I'm unlucky. And here comes Vernon to claim you."

He made her a small bow and departed. Diantha stared after him. For a moment it had almost seemed as if the earl would dramatically erase one of the other names and substitute his own. She was sure such a romantic gesture would be very uncomfortable, and she must be grateful that his lordship's sense of propriety had restrained him.

She allowed Vernon to lead her into the set, noticing, out of the corner of her eye, that Lord Chartridge had promptly solicited the hand of one of Vernon's numerous sisters. A very dull female,

Diantha thought, squabby build and no countenance.

"This must be a happy evening for you," she said politely to her partner.

"It's beyond everything," he assured her. "Marcella is such a wonderful girl. . . ."

Diantha then endured a very boring half hour listening to a dissertation on Marcella's perfections, in which, she felt wryly, she'd come by her just deserts.

The evening proceeded. Diantha danced her way through her card until it was time for Major Lytham's waltz. She looked around for him but saw instead that Lord Chartridge was approaching her. "I know this dance belongs to my brother, Miss Halstow," he said. "But I persuaded him to yield to me. I assured him that you wouldn't object."

"But I do," she said with strong indignation. "Your brother is the hero of the hour, and to be seen on his arm must add to any lady's consequence. I shan't forgive you for depriving me of that honor."

"Then it was very wrong of me," he said gravely. "But what's to be done? As I have robbed him, the saucy fellow is now using his 'consequence' to rob some other man. Look."

She followed his gaze and saw that George had audaciously purloined Elinor's hand from under the nose of the gentleman to whom it rightly belonged. "You're right," she said with a little smile. "I must yield with a good grace."

"Then let us take the floor. The music is starting."

Diantha colored faintly. She'd never been "missish" about the waltz, yet at the thought of dancing in this man's arms she felt unaccountably shy. She reproved herself. Obviously her aunt's expectations had made her nervous, and that would never do. Her chin lifted. "Yes indeed."

He led her onto the floor and fitted his hand into the small of her back. The sensation was unnerving, but she forced herself to be calm. Unbidden images chased through her mind: that shameless creature in Hyde Park, her wet clothes clinging to her voluptuous contours, the intimate smile she'd exchanged with the man whose arm was about Diantha now. A wave of self-consciousness went through her and she fixed her eyes on a point over the earl's left shoulder.

"I'm afraid my brother and your cousin are rather taken with each other," Chartridge said apologetically. "I know that will displease you, but it need not. George falls in love very easily, but it comes to nothing."

She managed to laugh. "I assure you I'm not troubled. Elinor, too, is always losing her heart. Next week she'll lose it to someone else."

She spoke warmly and he gave her a searching look. "You speak as if you were fond of her."

"I am. Very fond indeed."

"Although she clearly doesn't subscribe to your own beliefs."

"I'm not so foolish as to expect that. I know the world will never think as I do."

"And the world's opposition merely confirms you in your own convictions," he hazarded. "The set of your chin tells me so. You won't lightly abandon your ideas, but perhaps you've adopted them too easily."

"No," she said, the shadow crossing her face again. "I have reason for my beliefs."

They danced in silence for a few moments. Then Diantha looked up into the earl's face and saw there a strange look, compounded of cynicism, weariness, and something else that she couldn't identify. There was an ironic curl to his lip, and she suddenly became blushingly aware of the low-cut bosom of her dress, below his gaze.

"He must have been a paltry fellow," Lord Chartridge said at last, with a little smile.

"Who?"

"Come, you're not the first young lady to forswear love. The reason is always the same. Some gentleman failed to come up to scratch. But your heart will mend. It always does, you know." With the faintest touch of a sneer he added, "Nothing lasts, I promise you."

Two spots of anger burned in her cheeks. "Your assumption, sir, is not merely mistaken, but vulgar. My heart has never been broken, or even engaged."

Chartridge raised a sardonic eyebrow. "Do you ask me to believe that you've never been in love, Miss Halstow?"

"It's true," she told him defiantly. "Why should you find it so hard to believe? You have an uncommonly high opinion of your own sex if you think no woman can remain heart-whole."

He flushed slightly. "You're mistaken. I've no very great opinion of my own sex, but I'm tolerably well acquainted with yours. Young ladies commonly fall in love all too easily—"

"Boasting, my lord?" she inquired in a silky voice.

The hands holding her tightened sharply. She danced on, conscious of the painful pressure of his fingers, but even more conscious that the hand in the small of her back had drawn her closer than was proper. His face had grown hard with anger as it looked down on hers. Diantha had a giddy sensation that the world was spinning past her at an accelerating rate.

Abruptly the earl relaxed his grip. She drew away slightly and resisted the temptation to wriggle her fingers where he'd crushed them. Chartridge's face had cleared, self-mocking humor driving out anger.

"Yes, I sounded like a coxcomb, didn't I? My apologies, ma'am. I wasn't boasting. I said young ladies fall in love easily, not that *I* was the object of their affections."

The words *But you are* scorched across her brain before she could stop them. *Your face is handsome and your form pleasing. Even I can recognize this, although I'm armored in indifference. How much more must my frailer sisters feel!*

Lord Chartridge continued, "Like yourself, I observe the follies of my fellow creatures but remain apart from them. I was merely puzzled as to where you learned so much good sense."

"I was born with a cold heart, I think," she said with a little laugh.

"Has any man ever declared his love to *you*?" he demanded suddenly.

"Why, to be sure, one or two have been brave enough to try. But they never tried a second time. I've discovered that gentlemen don't like to be laughed at."

"A deadly weapon," he conceded. "You have me in a quake. Be sure I shan't risk your scorn by making you a declaration of passion."

"You relieve my mind, sir," she responded demurely.

He gave a crack of laughter that made heads turn toward them, and dropped his voice to say, "Miss Halstow, you're a minx. Have you no thought for these gentlemen's feelings?"

"I have as little thought for them as they have love for me," she returned. "Not one of them feels a particle of true emotion. They're moved by other considerations."

"You refer to your fortune," the earl said coolly. "But your looks are passable and you needn't despair of receiving an offer for yourself alone. However," he continued, ignoring her indignant gasp, "such an offer would doubtless be unwelcome to you, since it would spring from those tender feelings you so rightly despise. Clearly you're destined to be an old maid."

Diantha's lips twitched in appreciation of these tactics. "Not at all," she said. "My requirements in a husband are very particular, but I don't despair of their being met. Surely liking and respect aren't too much to ask?"

A cold look came over the earl's face and he spoke with an effort. "You're mistaken, Miss Halstow. Liking and respect are the rarest of all qualities between men and women. What woman could respect her husband if she knew half his activities? What man could respect his wife if he knew half her thoughts?"

Something in his voice made her ask quickly, "Has your experience of women's thoughts been so bad?"

"It's been damnable!" he said with bitter emphasis.

She met his eyes and saw that they'd darkened with emotions that had no place in her pleasant world. Yet she recognized them. She'd seen them in her mother's eyes long ago when news had arrived of some further exploit of her father's. Alva had poured out her woes without restraint, and her little daughter had heard much that she should have been spared.

Bitterness, rage, even hate: Diantha saw all these briefly reflected in the earl's glittering eyes.

Then the moment passed. He was himself again, smiling and saying civilly, "It was unpardonable of me to speak so. My feelings aren't as cool as yours. They sometimes get the better of my manners. I should have known—but no matter. The music is ending. Shall I take you to your aunt?"

"If you please."

He led her to where Lady Gracebourne was sitting with the chaperons. He remained a few minutes, exchanging polite commonplaces, then bowed and took his leave, including Diantha in a general glance.

It was four o'clock by the time she was in bed, and before she could blow out the candle Elinor put her head tentatively around the door. "Come in," Diantha said with a chuckle. "I'm longing to hear all about Major Lytham." She held back the sheet and Elinor climbed into bed with her.

"Oh, Diantha, didn't you think him handsome?" Elinor demanded as they snuggled down together.

"No, not a bit," Diantha said provocatively. "But I thought him exceedingly pleasant."

"Oh yes, and so much more. He said . . ."

She continued bubbling in this vein until Diantha said, "Dear Elinor, you make me worried. I hope this will be as fleeting as your other loves, for I'm sure my aunt and uncle don't plan to match you with a penniless younger son."

"Mama and Papa have only one match on their minds at the present," Elinor said, skillfully changing the subject. "And that's yours to Lord Chartridge. Did you like him?"

"Of course I did. His manners are gentlemanly and his person distinguished."

Elinor cried out on her for such moderate praise, adding, "You're such a strange creature. Whatever your feelings, I daresay you'd never admit them, even to yourself."

But here she did her cousin an injustice. Diantha was too honest to deny to herself that she'd been pleased with Lord Chartridge. When Elinor had gone she relived the evening and admitted that there was nothing in his form or behavior to disgust her. On the contrary, there was much to win her commendation. She believed his understanding to be superior and his disposition good. Most men of her acquaintance would have had no answer to the things she'd said to him, but he'd borne her attacks well and rallied quickly to give her her own again. It might be agreeable to be married to a man to whom one could speak frankly.

But then she recalled the black glitter in his lordship's eyes as the waltz ended. For a brief moment she'd glimpsed something dark and unpredictable, and now an inner voice whispered that this man might be moved by forces she'd never met before. The thought intrigued but didn't dismay her.

She lay for a long time, staring into the darkness, wondering what the future held.

Chapter Three

For four days there was no sign of Lord Chartridge. Diantha had almost given up hope of him when she was sent for one morning, and walked into the drawing room to find him, splendid in buckskin breeches and riding boots, with Lady Gracebourne. He made her a fine bow as her aunt looked up, a trifle flustered.

"My love, Lord Chartridge has been telling me of your conversation at the ball the other night," she said. "I'm afraid you let your lively tongue run away with you."

"I've told Lady Gracebourne how you insulted me," Chartridge said with a smile.

"I—insulted you?" Diantha echoed carefully. She was making a rapid mental review of the things that had passed between them at the ball and could think of none that she would care to have repeated to her aunt.

"To be sure, you did. You cast aspersions on my knowledge of horseflesh. I've come to make you unsay those words. You won't despise me when you've sat behind my bays."

He indicated the window, and Diantha hurried over and pulled back the lace curtain. In the street outside a small tiger was walking a pair of the finest matched bays she'd ever seen, harnessed to a curricle. Lord Chartridge came and stood beside her.

"I have permission to take you driving in the park," he said. His eyes teased her as he added too softly for Lady Gracebourne to hear, "If you care to risk yourself in the company of one who bishops his horses."

"You didn't tell my aunt that I said that?" she demanded, aghast.

"No, I merely reported the gist of your remarks. I spared her the actual text in case it gave her a spasm. But those are *my* horses, not my uncle's."

"They're a fine pair," she agreed. "It would be a pleasure to ride behind them. But I must change," she added, raising her voice and turning back into the room.

"Hurry then, my love," Lady Gracebourne said. "Lord Chartridge will not forgive you if you keep his horses waiting."

Diantha sped from the room and was back in twenty minutes in a dark blue walking dress with a cheeky little hat adorned with curling feathers and worn atilt. Chartridge said nothing, but his eyes told his admiration. He bid Lady Gracebourne farewell, promised to take good care of his charge, and escorted Diantha outside. The tiger held the animals steady while the earl helped her into the curricle. Then he took his place beside her and gave his horses the office to start.

The sight of the bays with their broad chests, powerful hindquarters, and elegantly arched necks brought home to Diantha the enormity of her crime. A man who could select these sweet goers and handle them with such strength and delicacy was a nonpareil indeed. They were fresh and fiery that morning, but silken mouthed, and they responded easily to the earl's dexterous handling.

He drove them well up to their bits, seemed untroubled by the heaviest traffic, and took his corners to an inch. Even when the bays took skittering exception to a tilbury driven by a gaudily dressed gentleman, Lord Chartridge controlled them without fuss, and passed the tilbury by sliding through a seemingly impossible space. Diantha wondered if he was displaying his prowess for her benefit, and when she saw him glancing at her from the corner of his eye she was sure of it. She burst out laughing and he joined her. They were still laughing as he swung around the corner and through the Apsley Gate into Hyde Park.

When they were a little way inside Lord Chartridge drew up and called out, "All right, Joe." The tiger immediately leapt to the ground and the curricle moved off without him.

"Forgive me for doing that without first seeking your permission," Chartridge said, "but I must speak with you privately, and I could think of no other way that wouldn't occasion comment."

"Won't this occasion comment?" Diantha asked as he tipped his hat to a passing lady.

"Not at all. One may be very private under the eyes of the whole world. Even without my tiger there'll be no talk as long as we circle the park no more than once. At a moderate pace that gives us perhaps twenty minutes, so I'll waste no time."

"You have all my attention, sir," Diantha said after waiting a moment, for it was clear that he had trouble in continuing.

Chartridge scowled. "Dashed if I know how to say it now. It seemed so easy when I—oh, the deuce! Miss Halstow, I must warn you of something of which you are clearly unaware. Our meeting the other night was no accident. Our friends have set themselves to promote a match between us."

"Oh yes," she said calmly. "I knew that."

"You knew?" Briefly he turned his head to stare at her.

"Of course. Why were you so sure I didn't?"

"Because," he said, startled into speaking frankly, "you went out of your way to provoke and anger me."

"And you would have expected me to simper and throw out lures to attract you?"

There was a brief pause before his lordship said in a voice of deep mortification, "You delight in making me sound like a coxcomb, ma'am."

Diantha's lip twitched. "Oh, no," she said gently. "It is not *I* who does that."

The silence grew sulfurous. Then, unexpectedly, Lord Chartridge began to laugh. It was a genuine laugh, full of amusement and without a trace of irony. "I exposed myself dreadfully, didn't I?" he said.

"You were a little incautious," she agreed in a friendly voice. "How unkind of me not to simper and flirt! But you know, I couldn't make myself do it."

"In fact, you were trying to put me off," he suggested lightly.

"Neither to put you off nor to lure you on. I was too angry with you to care if I offended."

"Angry with me? Why?"

Diantha chuckled. "Because you slighted me. I knew you were looking me over, and when you only awarded me one miserable little country dance I was furious."

"That settles it. Now you definitely think me a coxcomb."

"No. You've sometimes seemed determined to convince me that you were, but I have the strangest feeling that you're not."

"Thank you, Miss Halstow. Do you know, you're

the most extraordinary person. There isn't one young lady in ten thousand who'd have admitted to me what you just have."

"And of course, I shouldn't have done," she said ruefully. "Well, I told you I wasn't clever enough to keep my thoughts to myself. I'm frank to a fault. I always have been."

"And I told you that it wouldn't frighten away a man of sense. I prefer frankness to simpering. If you'd thrown out lures, I'd have fled the ballroom."

"Yes, I imagine you've had quite a few lures thrown out since your circumstances became known," she said calmly. "Now, don't poker up. You made a most unhandsome reference to *my* circumstances the other night."

He relaxed his countenance with an effort. "I suppose that's fair," he said reluctantly. "But you can't imagine how painful it is to me to find all my friends and relatives trying to turn me into a fortune hunter."

"No more painful than it's been for me to know that *my* friends and relatives study every gentleman I meet to see if he's what they consider my fortune merits," she returned.

"Yes, we're in something of the same case, aren't we? Then I needn't scruple to tell you that when I went to Allwick House the other night I had no idea you'd be there."

"And I thought you went to look me over," she said wryly.

"Not a bit. It's true I feared to find some heiress or other because my friends are so assiduous in casting them in my path, despite my protests. But if I'd known that *you* would be there, I wouldn't have gone. There's plain speaking for you."

"Because I've come into the Halstow banking fortune?" she asked lightly.

"I could have no other reason for avoiding you," he said in a gentler voice. "When we were introduced I resolved to do my duty and depart. But you're not quite in the common run of heiresses. In fact, you're not in the common run of young ladies. There were times during that waltz when I regretted that I hadn't followed my first instinct and left. You made me angry, but I found, when anger had died, that you also commanded my liking and respect." He said the last words slowly.

Now Lord Chartridge had yet another chance to discover how different was Miss Halstow from any other young lady. Instead of being discomposed by the significance of these words, she answered with a twinkle, "Enough for you to forgive me for being an heiress?"

"Enough even for that," he said. "I hadn't thought it possible, but your fortune no longer looms in my mind as a barrier to all honest speech. But now you must say something. If my words evoke no response, then I've made myself absurd to no purpose."

"You're not in the least absurd. You haven't committed the ultimate foolishness of declaring yourself in love with me, and I'm persuaded you never would."

"You're quite safe," he said gravely. "I'm past the age of folly."

"And I," she said in a voice that fell strangely on his ears, "have always been past the age of that particular form of folly."

He glanced at her, frowning a little. "If folly is unknown to you, how can you be certain that you're armored against it?" When Diantha remained silent he added, "I promise to respect any confidence you place in me."

"Thank you. I do trust you," she said after a moment. "You see, Lord Chartridge, my parents made a great love match, so I've heard. But by the time I was old enough to understand what I saw, they could no longer endure each other. They're dead now, both of them," she finished abruptly.

"Your experience has been sad. But are you wise to judge by only one couple?" he asked, his eyes fixed on his horses.

"It isn't only one couple. Perhaps the experience of my parents left me a little more observant than most girls. I look at those around me and see that romantic love had played them false." Diantha hesitated, then continued with a little constraint, "You must have observed the same. There are so many couples—"

"I'm slightly acquainted with your cousin Charlotte's husband," he said, showing a quick understanding that earned her gratitude. "He's a good fellow in his way, but with unfortunate manners."

"Manners?" Diantha echoed in surprise, for Lord Farrell was famed for the elegance of his address.

"I consider that for a man to expose his wife to society's derision by his infidelity betrays a shocking want of breeding."

Diantha nodded eagerly. "And it often seems to me that those couples who married in an excess of love are the first to . . ." She hesitated.

"The first to forget the obligations of love," Chartridge finished for her.

"That's exactly what I meant," Diantha said gratefully. "Oh, how I wish I were a man and needn't guard my tongue for fear of being thought unladylike!"

"Are you guarding it?" Chartridge asked with an air of surprise. "I must be very unobservant."

She gave a little choke of laughter. "I'm *trying* to guard it, but I keep forgetting."

He was entirely to blame, she thought, for having a mind so in tune with her own that nothing she could say shocked him. The wretched creature appeared to understand her only too well, for he immediately said, "I hope you won't guard it now. Only frankness will serve us. We'll soon be in sight of the Apsley Gate, and have very little time left. I must set the position before you in stark terms. You know that I've recently inherited my uncle's debts as well as his title, and must marry money in order to keep Chartridge Abbey and the estates. When my friends thought of a match between us they saw only the benefits to me. Clearly they gave no thought to you, otherwise they might have wondered why you should accept a man that you don't love and who comes to you encumbered by debt."

"I daresay they thought I'd be ambitious to be a countess," Diantha said lightly.

"And are you?"

She considered this for a moment before saying, "Will you think badly of me if I say yes?"

"I should think it strange if *you* were to say yes," he said thoughtfully. "Are you dazzled by a title? You'll find it a hollow thing."

"Not for me. I might begin to feel safe."

This was so totally unexpected that he stared at her.

"You see," she went on, "my parents *weren't quite the thing*, especially my father, who died in some way that no one ever talks about. I know he gambled shockingly, for my mother told me so, and when we heard of his death she said, 'I suppose he got into a quarrel with another cardsharp and came off the worst,' in a voice of such dreadful bitterness that I've never forgotten it."

Out of sight she twisted her fingers together in agitation. "I've had it drummed into me that I was balancing on a knife edge because of my parents, and so I must be twice as blameless as any other young lady. Sometimes it's seemed to me that I was living in prison because of someone else's crime."

There was a desperate note in her voice that made the earl say gently, "My poor girl."

"And it's crossed my mind," she went on, trying to sound unconcerned, "that there'd be a kind of safety and—and freedom—in being a countess. I wouldn't have to be always worrying in case I was judged 'not quite the thing.' "

"I can think of several countesses who are 'not quite the thing,' " Chartridge said wryly.

"Yes, so can I," Diantha said before she could stop herself. Then she hurried on, "But I've often thought that if I had . . . an assured position, the past would have less power over me. People might forget that I was the daughter of parents who weren't acceptable, and remember only that I was the wife of a man who *was*." She fell silent, for she was trying to put into words feelings she'd never needed to analyze before. But once again the earl obligingly came to her rescue.

"Yes, I think you've assessed the situation very astutely," he said in a voice that contained nothing but sympathetic understanding. His eyes gleamed suddenly. "And of course, the—er—freedom permitted a countess is far greater than you now enjoy."

"Is it really?" she asked with a touch of wistfulness.

"To be sure. It's the height of bad form for husbands and wives to live in each other's pockets, or to interfere with each other's rational amusements. Fidelity, not dependency, should be our motto." Then the laughter faded from his face and his voice became graver than she'd heard it yet. "The Apsley

Gate is in sight. We've talked as long as we dare. In sober earnest, Miss Halstow, do I have your consent to speak to your uncle?"

Suddenly it seemed that the bays were flying along, speeding her to the moment of decision that would plunge her into an unknown future. She'd vowed not to base her life on transient emotions, but was her own course any wiser? She hardly knew this man.

Lord Chartridge began to draw reign. The curricle slowed almost to a standstill. Diantha clasped her hands more tightly in her lap, took a deep breath, and said, "In sober earnest, my lord, you do."

When they reached Berkeley Square the door was opened to them by Ferring, Lord Gracebourne's massive butler. In common with all the other servants he knew what was afoot and regarded the lovers (for so he supposed them to be) with a benevolent eye.

"Is Lord Gracebourne at home?" Chartridge inquired, following Diantha into the hall.

Ferring's chest swelled with pride. "He is, my lord."

"Be so good as to tell him that the Earl of Chartridge would be grateful for a few moments of his time."

"Certainly, my lord. Would your lordship care to wait in the library?"

"Thank you." Lord Chartridge's voice was formal as he bowed to Diantha and said, "While I wait, Miss Halstow, perhaps you could find the book you promised to lend me."

Ferring's bosom heaved with indignation at this unloverlike speech. But his romantic soul would have been soothed if he could have seen what happened as soon as he'd departed. For the earl moved swiftly to shut the library door, and when they were alone he said in a low, urgent voice, "There's still time for you to cry off. I can invent some other excuse to speak to your uncle."

She stared at him. "Do *you* wish to cry off, my lord?"

"Miss Halstow, I'll be frank with you. We've discussed all manner of things this morning, to find out if we'll suit each other. But there's something we haven't considered, and it must be done before you commit yourself."

"What is it?" she asked, bewildered.

He hesitated. "You're so young," he said at last, "and for all your wisdom, so innocent. Marriage is a closer relationship than any you've known. It brings an intimacy that you can't imagine. It would be a tragedy for you to find yourself married to a man for whom you had an aversion."

Her cheeks flamed, and it was only with an effort that she managed to speak calmly. "Lord Chartridge, what . . . are you suggesting?"

A little smile touched his mouth. Something about it made her heart begin to beat with apprehension. "A rational experiment, madam," he said softly. "Which, with your inquiring mind, I know you'll approve."

"But—" she looked at him in bewilderment "—how can we possibly—?"

"Like this," he said, and swept her into his arms.

The floor rocked beneath her. Her hands, which had been raised instinctively to push him away, clung to him instead for support. His arm was curved beneath her neck so that her head was perforce flung back against his shoulder, her mouth raised helplessly to his. No man had ever kissed her in this way before, and the feel of his lips on hers astounded her.

More bewildering still was the awareness of his other arm in the small of her back, pulling her soft body against his big, powerful one, with a shocking disregard for propriety. She found herself held against him so closely that she could feel the heat of his flesh communicating itself to hers, and she was dizzyingly aware of the thin layers of material that were all that lay between his hand and her nakedness.

This was totally unlike the sedate clasp of the waltz, which, in her ignorance, she'd thought resembled an embrace. This was a ruthless assertion of power, but power of a new kind that she'd never dreamed existed. She'd known Lord Chartridge as a gentleman. Now she began to perceive that to know him as a man would be entirely different.

His lips were firm and warm as they caressed hers. She didn't know that her own lips had moved softly against his, and that her hands had clasped his body in a manner that was almost a plea. She was beyond conscious thought, beyond anything but the awareness of pleasurable warmth that was stealing over her. It weakened her will, making it impossible for her to struggle free and upbraid him for his ungentlemanly conduct, as she knew she ought.

Gradually she became aware that her mouth had been released and his arms were holding her less tightly. She was breathing quickly and scarcely dared to look at him for fear of what her flushed face would reveal. But when she did steal a glance upward she found that there was nothing to fear. He seemed totally in command of himself, which surprised her after the alarming impression he'd given of being about to abandon all restraint. She was too inexperienced to notice the little pulse throbbing slightly at the corner of his mouth. She only saw the laughter in his eyes, and realized with relief that it was kindly laughter. "Well, Miss Halstow," he teased. "Do you consider the experiment a success?"

She discovered that he was still holding her and drew away, a little flustered. But she managed to regain some of her composure and say in a light voice, "If I knew what you considered a success—?"

"Have you reached a verdict? Or shall we try the experiment again?"

"No," she said hastily, knowing that she needed time to come to terms with the new sensations coursing through her. "There's no need. I—I feel no aversion."

"Nor I," he assured her. "Forgive me for taking you by surprise, but these matters are best determined by—shall we say—instinctive reaction? Otherwise, it wouldn't have been a truly impartial experiment."

"Then you did the right thing," she assured him, her solemn manner at variance with the mischief in her eyes. "There's much to be said for rational inquiry."

Lord Chartridge took her hand and raised it to his lips. "Miss Halstow," he said gravely, "you're a philosopher."

Lord Gracebourne, hurrying into the library a few minutes later, found that his butler hadn't misled him. Diantha and the earl were seated at a proper distance, discussing the works of Shakespeare with as much cool civility as if they'd been married a year.

Within two days the *Gazette* and the *Morning Post* carried the news of the Chartridge-Halstow betrothal. To a man, the Chartridge creditors relaxed, and several final demands for payment were torn up almost at the moment of being sent.

There followed some cautious haggling between lawyers. Lord Gracebourne reported that Chartridge was behaving most oddly. "Considering the rank and dignity he's bestowing, he could have held out for twice what he's getting," he told his lady. "But he seems to want to receive as little as possible."

"Perhaps he's secretly in love with Diantha after all," Lady Gracebourne suggested sentimentally.

"For pity's sake, don't let her hear you say that," he begged in alarm. "It would be enough to make her call it off."

He conscientiously reported the negotiations to his niece, who came to realize that she would have a good deal of her fortune left in her own hands. She'd barely needed to consider money before, but now her wealth seemed all of a piece with the greater freedom that was opening before her. She was exhilarated with the prospect of that freedom, and the vista of her new life dazzled her. Marriage to a sensible man who would free her from constraints and cast his protection over her actions and utterances must surely be the most delightful state on earth. She listened politely while Lord Gracebourne discussed settlements, but finally begged him to say no more, adding, "I'm sure your arrangements for me will be excellent, Uncle."

This response struck him as entirely proper in a female, but so unlike his headstrong niece that he later asked his lady if Diantha was feeling poorly. Lady Gracebourne retorted that this was impossible. Diantha had only just returned from a ride with Lord Chartridge, her cheeks glowing with the exercise and her eyes alight with something that might have been pleasure in her fiancé's company, if anyone had dared to suggest it.

In fact, Miss Halstow had just put her new liberty to the test by galloping hell-for-leather in Hyde Park, a procedure guaranteed to incur the censure of the severe. But Chartridge, mounted on his glorious black stallion and gallantly keeping pace with her, had merely grinned and inquired, "Testing your new wings already?"

"Yes, don't my shocking ways alarm you?"

"I think my courage won't fail at the fence."

"Then I must find something much worse," she teased.

"You have me in a quake. But wait until we're married before you really set the town by the ears."

She'd laughed at this and they'd returned home in perfect accord.

This was almost the only private conversation they had in the rush of preparations for the wedding. She must inspect Chartridge House, choose her boudoir, and indicate how she desired it redecorated. She must receive visitors, for no member of Rex's family wished to be thought behindhand in paying her the proper attention. And if those visits were inspired as much by curiosity as by goodwill, they were still made with all proper decorum.

In addition Diantha must select a vast quantity of clothes. The best warehouses were visited, in the company of her aunt and cousin, and frequently when Lord Chartridge and Major Lytham came calling in the evening they found all three ladies worn to shreds, reclining on sofas, which amused them very much.

Diantha was able to acquit Chartridge of any loverlike behavior. He continued to act like a man of sense. His conversation was witty and he seemed to enjoy making her laugh. On the surface all was light and agreeable. But once she found him regarding her with an intensity that reminded her of those few flaming moments in the library, moments when the earth had rocked beneath her and she'd emerged to find the world a different place. She felt her color rising, and after a moment she turned away.

He followed her to the window, asking lightly, "Have I offended you?"

"No I—I feel suddenly tired."

He said what was proper, led her to a seat, and went to fetch her an ice. She used his absence to try to compose herself. Even more strongly than his kiss, she recalled him saying that his experience of women had been "damnable." Dark undercurrents swirled beneath their pleasant relationship, and suddenly her approaching marriage seemed more than merely a matter of freedom and pleasure. But when he returned his face had been wiped of everything save the faint ironic smile that she usually saw, and he made her laugh with a quip about their host.

Their honeymoon was to be spent at Chartridge Abbey. Rex had suggested a trip to the continent, now safe for travelers after Napoleon's defeat, but Diantha was eager to see her new domain, and a shrewd instinct told her that Rex wanted to put in hand certain necessary repairs to his ancestral home. So it was decided that the happy couple would travel to Kent to sojourn at the Abbey for two weeks before returning to town for Diantha's presentation at court.

Two days before the wedding a wagon set off from Gracebourne House bearing trunks full of the future Lady Chartridge's new wardrobe, to be taken to Chartridge Abbey. Only ignorant persons, of course, would believe that this represented the whole of my lady's equipage. During the honeymoon large numbers of gowns, including a court dress, would be delivered at Chartridge House in London, to await her arrival, and her subsequent descent upon the social scene in her new glory.

The wedding was the event of the season. Sticklers might consider that it ought to be a quiet affair, owing to the recent death of the late earl and his son, but there were so many with the right to be invited that it was clear the church would be packed. Just in time it was remembered that the present earl had been on only distant terms with his uncle and cousin, and therefore there need be no constraint on enjoyment.

A week before the wedding Diantha received the Chartridge pearls, consisting of a necklace, bracelet, and eardrops, from her groom. To these he added his own wedding gift of a matching pearl tiara. She exclaimed with delight, picturing the set with her bridal attire, in the event it lived up to her dearest hopes. The pearls were ideal with the white satin and lace of her wedding gown, and the tiara secured the veil to perfection.

She looked a vision as she stepped from the carriage outside St. George's, Hanover Square, and took her uncle's arm. Elinor was her attendant, charming in cream satin adorned with pale yellow rosettes down the front. She straightened Diantha's gown, and they were ready.

Their progress down the aisle was slow and stately. Diantha observed that the church was full before fixing her gaze straight ahead at the altar. One or two individuals stood out in the crowd. There was Bertie, killingly beautiful in dove gray garments that had made his tailor weep with joy, despite the bill that would never be paid.

As she neared the altar she saw George, Rex's groomsman, bestowing the briefest look on the bride before glancing over her shoulder to seek Elinor. And there was Rex, his face paler than she'd ever seen it. For once there was no irony in his expression. He seemed almost to be frowning as she neared him, and for a dreadful moment she wondered if he was regretting the whole business. But then his eyes softened as they rested on her, and she realized that his gravity wasn't caused by disapproval but by tension. The vicar appeared and they stood before him, side by side.

As the words of the marriage service rolled over Diantha, her mood of exultation over the thrilling future evaporated. Suddenly she understood what she was doing, giving her life into the hands of a man who was essentially a stranger. She'd mocked love, but without it there was nothing to unite them, save Reason. And for the first time she wondered if Reason was enough.

Then she felt the pressure of Rex's hand, urging her to meet his eyes. She did so, and was instantly flooded with reassurance. The world vanished. All that remained was this man, the disquieting sensations that flooded her at his touch, and the unknown life to which he was taking her.

And then it was over. The wedding ring was on her finger, the organ pealed out overhead, and she was returning back along the aisle, Lady Chartridge.

By early evening the earl and his new countess were ready to leave for the country. Rex had elected to drive her in his curricle, without his tiger in attendance for once. Diantha hugged her family farewell. Then she was up beside her lord; Chartridge took the reins into his hands and gave his horses the office to start.

For the first part of the journey they were largely silent. Diantha was enjoying the demonstration of skill that Rex's passengers always received. It was doubly in evidence on this journey, for he'd harnessed four horses instead of the more usual two, and he managed both wheelers and leaders with perfect ease. She watched his hands on the reins, large, shapely hands, created for subtle control. She couldn't take her eyes from them, even when Rex spoke, forcing him to address her twice.

"I beg your pardon," she said, startled.

"I asked if you were warm enough. There's an evening breeze springing up, I fancy."

"Quite warm enough, I thank you. Besides, it isn't far now, surely?"

"About an hour to Chartridge Abbey." He added, half to himself, "It will feel strange to go there as the owner."

"Have you lived there much?"

"A few years, when I was a boy. My father was never at ease with children, so when my mother died George and I found ourselves dumped on the earl. He cared for children no more than his brother, but his wife looked after us. In some ways I think she found our company more congenial than that of her own son. Oliver was like his father, coldhearted and selfish, minding nothing but his own pleasure. Perhaps I shouldn't speak of them so, now they're so recently dead, but even then I was old enough to understand how my aunt was kept short of money for herself, while there was always enough for gaming, and new hunters, and my uncle's mistresses."

The bitter way he said the last words made her

look at him. "I daresay I shouldn't speak of such things to you," he said with a wry smile.

"We agreed not to guard our tongues with each other," she reminded him.

"We agreed that *you* need not guard your tongue with *me*."

"Well, in justice, my lord—" she said indignantly.

He grinned. "Very well. You're no schoolroom miss to be shielded from knowledge of the world. Which reminds me, I didn't see Farrell at our wedding."

"He spends all his time with his latest high flyer," Diantha said crossly. "Charlotte merely sighed and told me he'd sent his compliments."

"Then you'll understand about my uncle. He broke my aunt's heart with indiscretions that he didn't trouble to hide. Oliver was cut from the same cloth. Had he ever married, his wife would have endured much, but he put it off because he said he didn't care for the kind of feminine reproaches his father had been forced to endure. Perhaps you begin to see now why few people liked either of them, and there's very little grief at their passing." He added abruptly, "I'm sorry my aunt is no longer alive. She would have liked you."

The sun had set and the light was fading fast as they swung into the village of Wellhampton. At once a shout went up and suddenly there was movement all around. Someone seized a horse and galloped off into the distance.

"The villagers are our tenants," he explained. "By now the news of our arrival will be halfway to the Abbey."

Folk were coming out of their houses to stare at them. "Let them see you," Rex advised, slowing his horses. "They owe you much."

From then on they were surrounded by cheers.

As they left the village she found more men, women, and children lining the road. Some of them had flaming torches, which they held high, lighting the road to the Abbey. It was almost dark when she made out the huge wrought-iron gates in the distance, being hurriedly pulled open, and now Diantha could see that the lines of torches went on past the gates and right up to the ancient building beyond. The roar rose higher as they swept onward, and she felt the exhilaration begin to grow in her again. Here were no censorious voices warning her to caution because of her dubious ancestry. Here were people who approved of her, rejoiced at her arrival, because she was their savior.

The entire household was lined up outside the great entrance. As the curricle drew to a halt an imposing butler and a middle-aged woman stepped forward to greet them. Rex handed her down and said, "This is Lopping, my dear. And this is Mrs. Edwards, your housekeeper. Between them they keep Chartridge Abbey running smoothly."

Diantha responded graciously to the speeches of welcome from the butler and housekeeper, then realized that she must go along the line of staff like a general inspecting troops. Summoning all her composure, she performed her first duty as Lady Chartridge, and never afterward in her life did she forget those first flame-lit moments, surrounded by smiling faces.

"And now, my dear, it only remains for me to introduce you to your new home in the traditional way," Rex declared with a grin.

Next moment he'd lifted her shoulder-high in his powerful arms, and carried her across the threshold into Chartridge Abbey. And the cheers followed them all the way.

Chapter Four

Sitting at her dressing table later that night, Diantha barely recognized herself. The flush of triumph was still in her cheeks. The excitement had been with her all through her first meal with her newly wedded lord, seated decorously at opposite ends of the dining table. She'd had barely any appetite, but she'd drunk several glasses of wine. She wondered if she'd had too much, and if that was why her heart was beating so hard now.

The low-cut silk nightdress was unlike anything she'd worn before, revealing almost all of her bosom. Of course, she'd worn revealing dresses for dancing, but somehow this was different. Looking in the mirror, she could see the reflection of the huge four-poster bed, and a slight tremor went through her.

So far it had all been easy. She'd struck a bargain with a man she liked, her money for his title. But now there was another bargain to be fulfilled, and the path ahead was dark and unfamiliar. Only her husband could lead her along it, and now she realized how little she knew him.

There was a click as a door opened behind her, and she saw him appear in the candlelight. The dancing shadows made him seem much taller than usual, and his features were unfamiliar. He wore a long dressing gown with wide sleeves and a heavy velvet collar. Beneath it Diantha could see his nightshirt, slightly open, revealing a broad chest on which the dark, curly hair grew up to the throat.

She heard a faint chink, and saw, with an absurd sensation of relief, that he'd brought glasses and a bottle of champagne. "I thought we might drink a private toast to business well transacted," he said lightly.

"Business?" she echoed doubtfully. It was business, of course, but somehow the word had a doleful sound.

"Let's say, the day when we both achieved our heart's desire," he amended. "You gained your freedom, and I secured the freedom of Chartridge Abbey." He handed her a glass of champagne. "To the future we will make together."

As they toasted each other she met his gaze, and something she saw there riveted her attention. There was a burning heat in his eyes, which started far back and reached out to encompass her. She felt naked, as though the thin silk nightdress had vanished. When Rex set his glass down she set hers down, too, following his movements as though hypnotized. He caressed her face lightly with his fingertips, and it was as though a brand had seared her. He brushed his lips against hers so gently that they barely touched, but the sensation left her dizzy.

Like all unmarried girls, she'd heard vague rumors about the wedding night. Lady Gracebourne had declared that "gentlemen must be humored," and Charlotte had shrugged and said, "What a fuss! One soon ceases to care." But nothing had prepared her for the shocking awareness of being totally alone with an unfamiliar male animal, and completely in his power. So far Diantha had made the terms. But with Rex's ring on her left hand, everything was different. The husband was master. The wife was helpless. That was how the world went. Whatever had she done, rushing into this marriage?

Rex had drawn back a little and was regarding her quizzically. "You may remember that we once tried an experiment," he said, "and you assured me that you felt no aversion to me. I hope nothing has altered."

"No—that is—no. It's just that—"

"It's just that you don't know what to expect." He gave his attractive grin. "Don't worry. I won't turn into a monster."

The grin reassured her. He was Rex again, the man who laughed with her, and made the world into a safe, reassuring place. Seeing her smile faintly, he said, "Trust me. And never fear me. You're not afraid of me, are you?"

"Certainly not," she said, so indignantly that he laughed aloud, and leaned down to kiss her again. His lips were warm and full, pleasant against her own, and she kissed him back, but modestly and with some hesitation.

Then she felt his tongue seeking a way between her lips. The pressure was gentle, not forcing but urging, and she relaxed her mouth to admit him. New sensations were coursing through her, making her blood pound in her veins and her heart beat strongly. She felt as if her will were gradually melting, leaving her no choice but to respond to the flickering movements of his tongue. Wherever he touched her there was new delight.

While he kissed her his hands had begun to rove over her body, tracing the curves of her flesh, the narrowness of her waist, the swell of her hips. She felt self-conscious at being so exposed to him, for her aunt had reared her in the strictest notions of modesty. But awkwardness was swept away in the flood of intense physical pleasure that rose up in her. It was unlike anything that had happened before in her life and it shocked her. This was dreadfully improper and not, she was sure, what Lord Chartridge expected in his wife. But Rex himself seemed intent on making these things happen.

Perhaps, she thought wildly, he was testing her to discover if she knew how to behave decently. In her ignorant state, anything seemed possible. So she fought to hold the pleasure down, or at any rate, not to reveal it too obviously. But it was difficult when her breath was coming in long, deep gasps, and every inch of her was trembling with the longing for something she didn't understand.

Rex began to slide his lips down the length of her neck to where a little pulse was beating madly at the base. The trail of sweet fire went on, over the swell of her breasts. Her heart was pounding madly as she felt his fingers drawing the nightdress down from her shoulders, down so that her breasts were completely exposed to his burning lips. She could feel herself blushing fiercely at this scandalous procedure. He *must* be testing her. No gentleman could seriously expect his wife to consent to such outrageous actions. It was time to prove to him that she was truly a lady.

From some far, reluctant place within her she summoned offended virtue, and pressed her hands against him. "No—Rex—no—please—"

He grew still at once, but continued to hold her against him. In the mellow glow of the candles she could see his face looking down on hers, and feel the trembling of his big body, as though he were holding himself in check with a mighty effort.

"Do you want me to go away, Diantha?" he murmured. "I told you, I'm not a monster. Say the word and I'll leave you to your chaste bed, and trouble you no more tonight."

The thought of his leaving her almost made her cry out. She didn't understand what was happening to her own body, she only knew that it was incomplete. He *must* bring this to a conclusion so that the sweet anguish in her flesh could cease to torment her.

But there were no words for a gently reared girl to say such things, and she looked at him in silent desperation.

"Do you want me to go, Diantha?" he repeated.

At last, inspiration came to her. "We made a bargain, my lord," she said breathlessly. "And—and I will not shun my duty."

His mouth quirked cynically. "Duty? An ugly word at the best of times, but especially now."

"But—but we agreed—" she stammered.

"Let's forget duty for a moment, and think only of pleasure. You haven't answered me. Shall I go?"

"I—"

"Shall I?" he repeated, brushing his lips softly over hers. "Your wish is my command. Tell me to go."

She couldn't answer. He was leaving a trail of fire down her neck, teasing her with movements so soft that she was hardly aware of them, except that each light touch made her head swim.

"Tell me to go," he whispered.

She could hardly speak, but she managed to murmur, "No—no—"

A drowsiness possessed her, as though she'd drunk some heavy narcotic. Her limbs were heavy. Her strength of will had simply vanished away. The whole world was changing around her and she was powerless to prevent it. Her nightdress whispered to the floor.

She caught a glimpse of two figures in the huge mirror. The candlelight threw flickering shadows over their bodies, and she realized that at some point Rex had discarded his clothes and was as naked as herself. Through her drugged delight she was awed by the beauty and splendor of him. The narrow hips and muscular thighs, so clearly glimpsed through his sodden breeches that first day in the park, were just as they had lived in her dreams. But now she could see clearly their steely power.

She felt herself lifted in his arms and carried to the great bed. Then she was lying down and he was beside her, kissing her everywhere, her mouth, her breasts, her belly, her thighs, until every part of her was hot with pleasure. As he kissed her he murmured words she could barely understand, the like of which she'd never heard before. She was no longer cool, collected Miss Halstow, who regarded the world from the safety of an amused distance. There was no safety in this man's arms, only delicious danger that thrilled her. She was a lady, reared in the rules of propriety and decorum. But now propriety was being thrown to the winds and she was coming alive as a woman.

She felt Rex's hand slip gently between her thighs, parting them. Before she had time to wonder what to expect, he had moved across her, between her legs. She was taken by surprise, but his face was there close to hers, smiling in reassurance. And the next moment everything in the world changed. She was no longer completely herself but a part of him, as he was part of her, joined in an intimacy that made her gasp with shock. Then the last tatters of her modesty were abandoned, and she was moving with him in a timeless rhythm that was beyond her own control.

She was possessed by pleasure, consumed by it, burned alive in its furnace heat. And, phoenix-like, from the ashes of her old self rose a new woman, joyful, and sensually awakened. She had discovered the world, and it was a glorious world, full of bright colors and glittering lights. She stretched out her arms, wanting it all, and felt herself showered with gifts from the gods.

It was over. As the flames receded she discovered that her body was no longer one with Rex's, but her own again, though changed forever. She was slipping down into warm darkness where there was the peaceful contentment of satiation. She fell at last into a blissful sleep.

In the last moments before waking Diantha had a dream in which she was held in Rex's arms, nestling against him as she slept, knowing that he was watching over her tenderly. She had a feeling of perfect well-being, of having come to the place where she belonged.

Then she awoke and found herself alone.

She sat up and looked around her. Only the rumpled appearance of the other side of the bed indicated that she hadn't been alone all night.

She threw herself back against the pillows as memory flooded over her. Shame scorched her as she remembered how wantonly she'd behaved, eagerly offering herself to intimate caresses and giving them back. After the first moment of amazement there'd been no virginal shrinking, none of the maidenly modesty that the Earl of Chartridge would expect of his wife on their wedding night. Instead, she'd forgotten her rearing and reveled in physical delight as totally as any courtesan. She burrowed under the bedclothes, thankful Rex wasn't there, and wondered how she could ever look him in the face again.

She heard the door click as Lucy, her maid, entered, and hastened to compose herself. Lucy beamed and set down the morning chocolate.

"His lordship has gone to the stables and begs you'll join him as soon as you've breakfasted," Lucy said.

Suddenly Diantha was galvanized into action. "Then pour my bath quickly, and lay out my riding clothes."

She hurried downstairs and out toward the stables. Rex was there, dressed for riding. He didn't see her coming, and she paused, half-hidden by a tree, and contemplated him. It occurred to her that he was a handsome man, his figure tall, lean, and hard. As she watched he suddenly burst into laughter at something said by a stable lad. It was a wonderful rich sound, and she felt her body tingle as though his laughter had the power to trigger hot memories.

As she approached he glanced up and saw her, and she had another shock, for his eyes held no awareness of what they had shared in the night. His greeting was pleasant, no more.

"Good morning, madam," he said, taking her hand and raising it to his lips. "I came out early to inspect your gift, and ensure that she was worthy of you."

"Gift?"

"Bring her out, Carter."

The stable lad snapped his fingers at someone inside, and the next moment Diantha cried out in delight at the sight of a charming, milky white mare.

"She's fast and spirited, but gentle as a lamb," Rex assured her. "The jewels were a formality. This is my true wedding gift."

Diantha ran her hands lovingly over the mare's velvety nose. "Oh, Rex, she's beautiful," she breathed. "I can't wait to ride her."

"Let's go at once."

He waved Carter aside and put out his hands to assist her to mount. Their eyes met. He was smiling in his old familiar way, and she understood. He wouldn't mention last night, and neither would she. It would be locked away in a private place where they could meet in secret.

He threw her up. His black stallion, the one she'd first seen him riding, was waiting there. Rex vaulted into the saddle, and the next moment they were away. She laughed as she felt the air whip past her face and the mare moving sweetly beneath her. The days of her restricted girlhood were over. She was free.

Diantha's notions of country life had been mostly formed in her childhood when she'd lived with her mother. Alva had bitterly resented her banishment, and found no pleasures in outdoor pursuits. Later when Diantha had gone to Gracebourne Park each winter she'd enjoyed riding and visiting the neighbors, but she'd never gotten deep into country pleasures.

But as the days passed at Chartridge Abbey she discovered that everything was different. She was the lady of the manor, patroness of the village. This was *her* countryside.

She gave a series of small dinner parties to meet the local gentry, the squire and his wife, the mayor, and Mr. Ainsley.

Mr. Ainsley was a local character of good blood, who'd inherited Ainsley Court, a small but delightful property that had been allowed to run down while he spent every penny on gambling. Its rents now brought in a pittance on which he and his one remaining servant subsisted, and it was an open secret that he shot game and fished the rivers in order to have enough to eat. He supplemented this diet by dining with his many friends, and taking home leftovers to feed his servant. Diantha had begun by expecting to dislike him, and ended up won over by his gentle charm. In an hour they were friends, and he slightly disconcerted her by asking if she would like to buy Ainsley Court.

"He asks everybody," Rex told her later. "He'd love to get it off his hands and buy a small annuity."

"It might be worth thinking about," she mused. "It adjoins our property."

"And it's in an even worse state. It would cost a fortune to bring it into order."

She made a mental note to consider the matter later, but in the riot of new interests it soon slipped from her mind.

On the first Sunday after their arrival Rex took her to morning service in the ancient little church at Wellhampton. The Reverend Dunsford was a thin, ascetic-looking man with gray eyes. He delivered the sermon in a gentle voice, behind which, Diantha suspected, was considerable firmness of character. She liked him, and Sophie, his softly spoken daughter. Sophie wasn't pretty, but her countenance was sweet and her manner quietly assured from having been mistress of her father's house since her mother's death, eight years earlier.

In due course they were invited to dine at the Abbey, and Diantha found her a charming companion, although alarmingly learned. Sophie had been her father's pupil and knew Latin and Greek.

"Papa said it would prepare me to be the wife of

a man in orders," she confided with Diantha while they were alone after dinner.

"Must you marry a man in orders?" Diantha asked, frowning.

"I know Papa hopes for me to wed a serious, godly man. He says anything else would lead to misery, and I know he's right." But then a gleam of fun lit Sophie's gentle eyes, and she admitted, "But I've had three offers, and though I wish to be a dutiful daughter, I simply *could* not accept any of them."

"Were they not serious and godly?" Diantha queried.

"Oh yes, all of them. But one of them was terribly fat, and one sniffed and had clammy hands, and the third one referred everything to his mother."

"Everything?" Diantha asked, awed. "I mean—matters of the church?"

"Everything," Sophie confirmed simply. "I once heard him say that his dear mother saw nothing to disapprove in moderate amusement, and it was also pleasing in the sight of the Lord. I fancy even Papa was relieved when I rejected him."

The two girls chuckled together, and were still laughing when the gentlemen joined them. Catching the end of their conversation, Diantha realized that they were discussing theology. Then serious matters were dropped to attend to the ladies.

"I never dreamed you were so learned," she said to Rex when he joined her in her room later that night. "Latin quotations! I thought you cared for nothing but sporting pursuits."

He shrugged. "A man must do a little work at Oxford. There's more to life than driving a curricle and pair through a narrow gate, or taking part in a mill. The vicar's a good fellow, isn't he?"

"Yes, I like him very much."

"He's distantly connected to Viscount Ellesmere, but you'd never know it to hear him talk."

"Unlike some others who would mention it at every opportunity," Diantha agreed. She, too, had met the kind of clergy, younger sons of younger sons, who'd entered the church for lack of talent for anything else, and supported their spirits by constant references to noble families who'd long forgotten them.

"I think he slightly disapproves of the Ellesmeres," Rex said with a grin. "They've invited him several times, but he finds the atmosphere of their house 'displeasing.' "

They laughed together, and he snuffed out the candle. Then he took her hand, drawing her to her feet to lead her to bed. It was always like that. In the darkness they met and mated on another plane, two different people from their everyday selves. He uttered no words of passion or tenderness, but after that first night he'd drawn her step by step into a world of hot sensuality where only actions counted. The respectable Lady Chartridge would know nothing of such a world, but Diantha reveled in it.

He would slip away when she was asleep. Sometimes she had the recurring dream that he lay with her enfolded in his arms, or kissed her as she slept. But she always awoke alone.

There were new interests to enliven her days. At her request Rex was teaching her to drive his curricle, and she pretty soon became adept at handling the ribbons.

"Bertie offered to teach me once," she told him, "but Aunt Gloria wouldn't allow it."

"If he drives no better than he rides, that's a tribute to her judgment," Rex said dryly.

"Oh, no, he's an excellent whip. He can even drive random tandem." She feather-edged a corner in style before asking naively, "Can you drive random tandem, Rex?"

One of the more notable sportsmen of his day suppressed his laughter long enough to answer, "I can just about manage it, m'dear."

Random tandem was an arrangement of three horses, with two harnessed side by side, and a third in front and center. It looked very dashing and was exceedingly difficult to handle. Diantha glanced at him and saw that his lips were quivering.

"I daresay that was very silly of me, wasn't it?" she asked.

"Just a little," he said kindly. "But if your cousin can drive that way, my opinion of him improves."

Next morning he had three horses harnessed and gave her a demonstration of his skill, which Diantha had to admit surpassed Bertie's by some distance.

"How I would love to drive this way," she said. "Do teach me."

"Not for a very long time," he told her firmly. "I don't choose to see my equipage on its side in a ditch."

"How ungallant you are," she complained. "But perhaps you fear for my safety?"

"Not at all. I fear for my horses' knees."

"Not even a little concern for your wife? Fie, sir!"

"Why should I be concerned? Whatever happened to you, there'd never be fewer than five of my staff eager to lay down their lives to rescue you."

This was a reference to a scuffle that had broken out in the stables only that morning over who was to have the privilege of holding Diantha's horse.

The new Lady Chartridge had wasted no time winning the servants over.

"But doesn't the thought of my pathetic lifeless form inspire you with a little pity?" she asked impishly.

"If you're fool enough to drive random tandem, you deserve to be lifeless," he retorted. "And stop flirting with me. I'm no lovesick stable boy."

She laughed aloud at that, and they finished the journey in harmony. But she discovered that she missed male admiration more than she would have thought possible. Declarations of passionate devotion would still have bored her, but the little stiletto thrusts of flirtation were another matter. Rex refused her even a modicum of gallantry. She didn't blame him for that, since she'd ordered him never to speak of love. But it had become a kind of game with her to see if she couldn't tease him into saying something chivalrous.

It piqued her slightly that she'd never succeeded, but she didn't brood. Rex had kept his part of the bargain admirably. An assured place in the world, and her freedom. She reveled in them both, but especially her freedom.

Her behavior grew more daring. When, in the privacy of their bedroom, she demanded one of Rex's cigars to smoke, he gave it to her without demur, and laughed heartily when she made a face and threw it away.

"If you want to set society on its ear by smoking in public, you'll have to develop a stronger stomach," he teased.

"I think I'll find something else," she said faintly.

But she didn't seek his approval the day she decided to ride Nestor, Rex's thunderous black stallion. Rex was away, having driven off in his curricle to visit some sporting friends, when she visited the stables, clad in her elegant black riding habit.

"You can throw my saddle over Nestor," she said carelessly to Tom Abelard, one of the stable lads.

Tom paled. He was a nice boy of eighteen with brown, honest eyes, who rushed to be the first to serve her. "Nestor, my lady," he gasped. "But he ain't a lady's horse. His lordship—"

"Has Lord Chartridge ever instructed you that I could not ride him?" Diantha asked.

"Well, no, not exactly, but—"

"Then please saddle him for me, without further delay." Diantha mitigated the severity of her words with a dazzling smile that completed the boy's demolition.

"Wh—what shall I saddle for your groom?" he asked.

"I shan't take a groom with me today," Diantha said. "Hurry now."

As soon as she was on Nestor's back she knew that this horse was different. A fierce thrill went through his sleek, muscular body, and another moment he was away. At first she managed him pretty well. He was strong and fresh, but so was she. But at last she began to tire. Her arms ached from the effort to keep him in control, and she could sense that he wasn't tired at all. At last came the moment she'd dreaded, when their wills diverged, and Nestor's will prevailed. If anything, his speed increased and she was being carried away, willy-nilly, by a beast with the power of a steam engine.

A stone wall appeared ahead of her. She gasped with horror, but the next moment they were over it, and flying on. She was truly afraid now, but she clung on grimly until another wall appeared. It was lower than the last, but she was exhausted and somehow everything slipped away from her. Mercifully the ground was soft when she hit it, but she landed hard enough to wind her. For a few moments she whooped and gasped until her breath returned, and she could sit up and see Nestor vanishing in the distance.

She got painfully to her feet, cursing herself for having let go of the rein. Not that holding on to it would have helped her much, she reflected. She couldn't have mounted Nestor again without help, and she wasn't sure that she wanted to. He would gallop home, and they would come for her. She only hoped Rex would know nothing about it.

But when she'd limped in a homeward direction for an hour, she knew that hope was in vain. To her incredulous dismay she could see a curricle that looked alarmingly like Rex's, appearing in the distance. And there, sitting in it, was her black-browed husband.

He drew rein and sat scowling at her. She wouldn't have believed he could look so angry. "You're on your feet, so I suppose you're not seriously hurt," he snapped.

"Yes, I'm well," she said breathlessly. "Bar a few bruises."

"Serve you right," he said savagely. "You deserve to have broken every bone in your body. How dare you take Nestor out!"

"He got back—?"

"Yes, he got home and threw everyone into a fright."

"Everyone except you, I feel sure," she said with spirit.

"Oh, I knew you'd be all right, you thoughtless little wretch. It's others who must suffer. Get in."

He reached out so that she could steady herself as she climbed painfully into the curricle. "What did you mean about others suffering?" she asked when they were moving.

"I mean Tom Abelard. He had no right to saddle Nestor for you."

"I ordered him to."

"He should have ignored you."

"You *told* him that he should have ignored my orders?"

"Of course."

"Pretty well to make a fool of me in my own home," she flashed.

"I'll forbear to make the obvious retort to that," he said grimly. "You knew you were doing wrong, else why did you wait until my back was turned? And Tom knew it, too. It leaves me no choice but to dismiss him."

She gasped with horror. "But you can't do that."

"That's precisely what I can do, madam."

"But it wasn't his fault!"

"That's unfortunate. I have to let the others see what comes of disobeying me."

"But he's got a widowed mother to support," she cried in horror.

"He should have thought of that. He leaves my employ, and they both leave their cottage."

She set her chin. "If you dismiss him, I shall rehire him for some other work. If I pay his wages, you'll have nothing to say."

Rex gave a short bark of laughter. "I'll have a great deal to say," he said grimly. "I warn you, madam, don't engage me in that sort of battle. You'll lose. You may be Lady Chartridge, but I am the earl, and my word is law, not yours."

Diantha stared at him, appalled at such a demonstration of cold power. This was Rex as she'd never known him, and it shocked her to think she'd tied herself for life to a man who could be so ruthless.

But she would worry about that another time. For the moment, saving Tom was what mattered. Like a great general coming about, she swiftly changed tactics.

"Rex, please," she begged. "Don't punish him for my crimes. I'll do anything. I'll never go near the stables again. I'll sit in my room and sew until we go back to London. I'll—" She stopped, for Rex had thrown back his head and bellowed with laughter. "What is it?" she demanded in outrage.

"The thought of you, tamely sitting in your room and sewing," he said in a choking voice.

"I mean it."

"I know you do. Diantha, you goose. As though I'd harm Tom, whose father taught me how to handle a gun, and whose mother used to feed me her apple pie! I've told him if he ever does such a thing again, I'll have the hide off him, but I've no intention of dismissing him."

"Then—it was all a pretense? How dare you!"

He grew serious again. "It was a valuable pretense if it taught you to think. If you'd broken your neck, you wouldn't have been the only one who suffered. Tom would have been in bad trouble. And think of me."

She eyed him cautiously, wondering if Rex actually meant to pay her a charming compliment. "You, my lord? Would you mind very much if I broke my neck?"

"To be sure, I would," he replied coolly. "I've married the Halstow fortune. Imagine what the world would say if my bride died within a month of the wedding—on my horse, too?"

"They'd call you a monster," she said, appreciating these tactics. "And I'm strongly of the same opinion."

"If you want to come to an early end," he told her cheerfully, "wait until you've presented me with an heir. Then he can inherit your fortune when I yield to an overwhelming impulse to wring your neck. The world will say I acted under provocation."

"Then my path is clear," she said gaily. "To protect my life I must immediately draw up a will making you my sole heir, ahead of any son."

"Never!"

The crack of Rex's voice was so harsh that Diantha stared. He pulled up sharply and turned to her, his face pale. "Never," he repeated. "On no account must you do such a thing."

"Rex, for pity's sake! I'm not really afraid for my life."

"It isn't that," he said. "Understand me, I have no desire to inherit your money. It's bad enough—" He checked and with an effort brought himself under control. "Give me your solemn word that you'll never do me such an injury."

"But—"

"Give me your word!"

"Very well. Whatever you wish. You have my word." She searched his face, whose pallor alarmed her.

He relaxed a little. "Let us speak of this no more. It's a subject I dislike." He started the horses, and remained quiet for the rest of the journey.

Diantha found Tom looking anxious. When he saw her safe a beaming smile broke over his face, and it brought home to her, even more forcefully than Rex's words, that she'd unforgivably embroiled him in her scrape.

Rex ordered her to bed and sent for the doctor, who prescribed a day's rest for her bruises. She spent it sleeping and brooding. Rex had reverted to his usual ironical self, but the mask had slipped, allowing her a brief glimpse of a man uneasy with his wife's vast wealth. He covered it with a smile, but it was there, almost shading into bitterness. Today had been a small but significant power struggle between a man proud of his heritage and the woman who he feared might try to lord it over him.

Only when he came to kiss her good night did she remember something that had struck her as odd.

"How did you come to be home so early, Rex? You were to be away all day and night."

"I turned back," he said grimly. "I had a presentiment of danger."

Diantha's bruises healed quickly, and within a couple of days she was in the saddle again, riding with Rex over their acres. Wherever they went she drew glances of admiration and, what was more important to her, approval. She was their countess. She'd saved them. At last she belonged.

But gradually she began to wonder just how effectively she'd saved them. Increasingly what she saw as she rode about wasn't merely a lower standard of living than her own, it was abject, terrifying poverty, filled with fear and the threat of illness.

"I told you my uncle was a coldhearted villain who spent every groat on his own pleasures, or his son's," Rex told her as they came out of some stinking hovel and took gasps of fresh air. "There are repairs here that should have been done years ago."

"They should have been torn down and rebuilt years ago," Diantha said with a martial light in her eye that her aunt would have recognized, but which Rex hadn't learned about yet. "We must do it at once."

"I intend to—or at least, as soon as possible."

"Why not at once?" she demanded.

When they had ridden halfway home she demanded again, "Why not at once?"

He made a wry face. "Have you any idea of the cost?"

"What does the cost matter?" After a few moment's silence she said, "Uncle Selwyn always said you wouldn't take enough of my fortune. You could have had twice as much."

"But I preferred not to," he said in a voice that set her at a distance. "Shall we gallop?"

He raced ahead, leaving her no choice but to follow. Diantha allowed the subject to lapse until late that night, after they'd returned from dinner with the mayor. As often before, Diantha waited for Rex, sitting at her dressing table, her golden hair streaming over her shoulders. But this time she was scribbling on a sheet of paper and didn't immediately notice his entrance. She shivered pleasurably as he kissed the back of her neck, but finished her writing.

"What can be of such consequence that it makes you ignore your husband?" he teased, looking over her shoulder. "Good God, what are all these figures?"

"I'm trying to work out what sum would be needed to bring the whole estate into good repair," she explained. "But it's hard because I don't know what things cost."

"So I imagine. Must you occupy yourself with this now?"

"Delaney would know, wouldn't he?"

"Delaney knows most things, but—"

"You could write to him tomorrow and tell him to come as fast as he can."

Rex sighed. "Can't you trust me to do my best for the tenants in my own way?"

She looked into his face. "You took too little from me, didn't you?" she accused. "My dowry won't begin to cover it."

"I took only enough to cover pressing debts," he admitted. "In fact, I hadn't been round the estate as thoroughly as you've done—"

"So you didn't know the need for these things. Otherwise you'd have accepted more."

"Perhaps, but—"

"Well, we can settle it very simply," Diantha said cheerfully. "I'll write to the bank about transferring funds to you. You'll need a great deal, and it may mean selling some—"

"Wait," he stopped her firmly. "I've taken as much money from you as I wish to."

"But that's the greatest absurdity. You said yourself you married the Halstow fortune, not for yourself, but for your dependants. To take less than enough would be nonsensical."

"There are some matters that I should prefer to take care of myself," he said firmly.

"But that will take time, won't it? Some of those places we saw today are death traps. That's why so many of their babies die. And more babies will die if we delay a moment longer than necessary. Rex, you *can't* let that happen."

After a moment's silence he gave a wry smile. "You're quite right, my dear. My pride isn't worth a single child's life. It must be put in hand immediately. Please send for Delaney and give him your instructions."

She frowned. Now she'd won the argument, she was also aware of having lost something. The next moment Rex kissed her cheek, murmured about her undoubted tiredness, and left the room, leaving her staring into the mirror, not at all tired, and horribly aware that she'd done the right thing in a clumsy way.

Next day Rex approached her with a smile, saying, "What a bear you've married! Try to forgive my ill temper. I'll send for Delaney today."

Delaney was with them within hours, riding beside them over the estate, fiercely making notes and doing calculations. When he presented Rex with his conclusions the earl passed the paper to Diantha with a shrug. She immediately wrote to her bank, instructing that the necessary funds should be credited to Rex, and the matter was concluded.

But there was something wrong with her triumph. A vague uneasiness nagged at her heart and wouldn't go away. When Rex declared it was time to return to London she agreed with relief.

Chapter Five

Their arrival at the house in Grosvenor Square was the start of the most exciting period of Diantha's life. Her new wardrobe had been delivered in her absence, including the magnificent gown for her court presentation. Luckily Diantha had the kind of tall, lissome figure that could support the hoops that etiquette decreed. Her only jewelry was the Chartridge pearls, with Rex's wedding tiara securing her three ostrich feathers.

"You look magnificent," Elinor breathed. "Positively regal." She had accompanied her mother to Chartridge House to enjoy the preparations.

"Let us hope not," Lady Gracebourne declared, surveying her niece critically. "Only the queen is allowed to look regal. To overshadow her, my love, would be a serious breach of etiquette."

Lady Gracebourne was herself wonderfully attired in deep blue satin, finished off with sapphires and diamonds, ready to sponsor Diantha for her debut into society, not as a green girl, but as an elegant young matron. She stood back to inspect her handiwork with satisfaction, knowing that her niece did her credit.

Rex appeared in Diantha's room and regarded his wife warmly. "Let's hope the Prince Regent isn't there," he said. "He has an eye for beauty and will certainly cut me out. Shall we go, my lady?"

As he led her downstairs George appeared through the front door, and stood gaping at his sister-in-law's splendor.

"Now, my love," Lady Gracebourne said, addressing Elinor. "Return home as soon as we've gone. Our carriage will be ready for you directly."

"I thought I would walk home, Mama," Elinor said with a casual air. "There are some shops I wish to visit."

"Not without your abigail," Lady Gracebourne said. "And she isn't here."

"If I may offer my services to Lady Elinor," George said quickly.

Lady Gracebourne consented and thanked him vaguely. It was clear her mind was on Diantha. A few moments later they were in the carriage and moving off. Diantha spared a moment's appreciation for Elinor's little stratagem, before turning her thoughts to her presentation at court.

Rex's hopes were fulfilled. The Prince Regent was not present at his mother's Drawing Room, but in every other way the event lived up to expectations. Diantha curtsied before Queen Charlotte, very plain but very majestic, and before the Princesses Elizabeth and Amelia, and later spent a gratifying amount of time engaged in conversation with them. After that her position was assured. Invitations jostled each other on her mantelpiece, and at a very grand ball given by Countess Lieven a few evenings later, she finally met the Regent.

He was a fat, florid man, held in by corsets that creaked, and reeking of perfume. But he behaved like a young beau, flirting outrageously with the new Lady Chartridge and virtually ignoring all the other women in the room.

"Shocking, madam!" Rex declared as they were riding home. "To dance with him three times."

In the dim light of the carriage Diantha could just make out the glint of humor in his eyes. She chuckled. "Now, how could I refuse the royal command? To be sure, I cared for it very little. I was half fainting from his scent."

"Should I have protected you more determinedly?"

"No such thing!" she said indignantly. "I can protect myself, my lord."

"I believe you can," he said, regarding her satirically.

Her diary filled up quickly. Balls, parties, routs—there wasn't enough time in the week for all the engagements that would be incomplete without her. There was no end to the pleasures that a dashing young matron could enjoy. It was she who now chaperoned Elinor to parties and visits to Almack's. Lady Gracebourne's attention was taken up these days with her youngest son, who showed a disposition to be sickly, and she was glad to delegate this duty to Diantha. Lord Chartridge usually excused himself from Almack's, preferring to blow a cloud with some friends at Cribb's Parlour, or visit a prizefight. But Major Lytham seemed to have lost interest in these pursuits, which would hitherto have absorbed him as much as his brother, and could always be relied on to squire the ladies.

Diantha was sure that marriage must be the most delightful state in the world, and Rex the perfect husband. His manner to her was pleasant and frequently he would make her laugh, but he didn't behave like an infatuated man. Even as a lover he was wry, courteous, and always a gentleman. He would come to her bed with a smile, blow out the candle, and take her into his arms. Then they would travel to that other dimension, where she was free to react with blissful pleasure to his caresses. But he would leave her soon afterward. They didn't sleep in each other's arms, and by day the matter was never mentioned.

Sometimes Diantha would look up to find him watching her intently, as though he were waiting for something. It gave her an odd sensation of disturbance, but if she ventured to question him, he always answered with a laugh. For the moment she was content to leave matters there. She was enjoying herself too thoroughly to look below the surface of her marriage.

As befitted a fashionable couple, they didn't live in each other's pockets. Rex took his seat in the House of Lords and became interested in politics. He also continued with his sporting pursuits, and as the year drew on he visited the country more often. He had no qualms about leaving Diantha alone as, like many ladies of rank, she'd quickly acquired a circle of admirers, who competed to escort her wherever she went.

One of these, to her great amusement, was the dangerous Lord Byron. Since she'd become all the crack, he paid court to her as a matter of form, for he hated to be behind the fashion. But Diantha had disconcerted him by refusing to swoon at his aura of romantic wickedness. She had even burst into giggles at one of his more passionate pronouncements. He'd stormed off in a huff, but returned next day with a poem dedicated to her.

"Which is more than he's ever done for Caro Lamb," Countess Lieven observed dryly. "They say she's fit to murder you. Well done, my dear. Continue to snub him. It will do him the world of good."

"And keep him knocking at my door," Diantha responded impishly.

Byron did more than knock at her door. At a ball given by Lady Castlereagh he leaned against the wall, glowering at Diantha in a passion of poetic torment. When she refused to sit out a dance in his company he smote his brow, and when she smothered a smile he cried, "You mock me, madam! Ah, but you shall see! Out into the night with me!" At that he strode out, leaving his hostess indignant and Diantha in gales of laughter.

Rex, who'd witnessed the scene, murmured in her ear, "A trifle vulgar, don't you think, madam?"

"Dreadfully," she agreed. "But very entertaining."

"How can you laugh at his broken heart?" Rex asked satirically.

"Fiddle! He has no more of a heart than I have. Oh, Rex, don't say I must drop him. None of the others makes me laugh nearly so much."

He regarded her with a strange look in his eyes. "Never fear. I'm not going to become a heavy-handed husband. After all, we agreed not to interfere with each other's rational amusements."

He'd swiftly grown used to returning to discover his home filled with nosegays and other tributes to his wife, but the fact seemed to amuse rather than disturb him.

"I see young Keswick's attentions have greatly increased," he observed one day. "Shall I need to call him out?"

Diantha chuckled. "Not at all. If there is any calling out to be done, I have three other gallant gentlemen ready to do it for me."

"You relieve my mind, m'dear. I was in a quake at the thought of facing him." Since Rex was a crack shot and Keswick a sentimental dandy, this remark made them both laugh.

"But you will take me to the queen's soiree next week, won't you?"

He grinned. "You mean to attend on your husband's arm? Fie, Diantha!"

"I know," she sighed. "Shockingly dowdy, ain't it? But then, the court *is* dowdy."

"I'd planned to go to the country the day before, but for your sake I'll delay my departure. How nice to know that you still have some use for your neglected husband."

Rex squired her to the queen's soiree, preserved a straight face while two princes competed for his wife's attention, and left for the country the following day. He kissed her cheerfully, advised her to "be good, and if not, be discreet," and swept off in his curricle, leaving her wondering if there was another husband like him in the world.

Instantly she plunged into a new round of gaiety. There were balls, routs, Venetian breakfasts. She watched a balloon ascension with Lord Keswick, and visited Bartholomew Fair with Lord Ashburn (or it might have been the other way around: she was fast losing track).

One night, as she was preparing for a ball at Almack's, trying to decide between diamonds and pearls, Eldon, her new dresser, entered with a sprig of flowers.

"White roses," Diantha exclaimed. "At this time of the year!"

The answer was to be found on the card. The roses came from Lord Spenlow, the youngest and most ardent of her admirers, and had obviously been culled from the famous Spenlow hothouses. Diantha studied them, her heart touched by their perfect beauty. Simon's youth sometimes led him to overstep the bounds of propriety, and she'd recently been compelled to snub him, for his own sake as much as hers. But she liked his frank, eager nature, and hated to hurt him. Tonight she decided she could risk a little kindness.

"Arrange them in my hair, please, Eldon," she said. "It will make a pleasant change from a tiara."

The result was all she could have hoped. The roses made her appear daringly different. Diantha was so pleased that she stripped off the rest of her jewelry and had the roses pinned over her shoulder and down her dress. Tonight she wore blue satin and silver lace, and the perfect white of the blooms made a dazzling impression.

She first directed her coachman to travel the short distance to Berkeley Square, where she would collect Elinor from Gracebourne House. Her cousin was radiant in cream satin, her mother's diamonds about her neck. But no diamond was brighter than Elinor's eyes. They sparkled with joyous anticipation of the evening ahead, and Diantha's heart sank, for she was sure she knew the reason. She hastened to tell Elinor that George was visiting friends in the country and not expected back for a week. Elinor's smile became brighter, but it had a fixed quality that made Diantha say, "Elinor dear, my aunt and uncle will never allow it."

Elinor blushed faintly but said, "You refine too much upon a mere flirtation. Just because I occasionally dance with Major Lytham—"

"I don't want to see your heart broken," Diantha said worriedly.

"George would never—that is, Major Lytham is a man of honor—"

"I know he is. But sadly, he has very little money."

"Papa and Mama would never hold that against him," Elinor said fervently. "Besides, as your brother-in-law, he's one of the family. How can they object?"

"As loving parents they will object to seeing you

married to a man who can't keep you properly," Diantha urged.

Elinor blushed again, and seemed to realize that she'd revealed too much. "There's no question of marriage," she said primly. "I assure you, you are refining too much on it."

With that Diantha had to be satisfied.

They arrived to find Almack's a blaze of light, with merry music that could be heard from the pavement. Diantha swept regally in, her eyes blazing with excitement as she surveyed the couples who dipped and swayed beneath the glittering chandeliers. In just a short time she'd made this her own domain. Several gallants detached themselves from the damsels who were trying to hold on to them, and made for her like arrows. She waited to see Elinor's hand safely bestowed on a middle-aged baronet, before plunging into a desperate flirtation with three of her admirers at once.

She had a thoroughly enjoyable evening, in the way she was now used to. Self-confidence had put a sheen on her beauty. Gallants swarmed about her, paying tribute. Unmarried girls regarded her jealously, and behind the fans chaperons gossiped that the young Lady Chartridge was slightly scandalous. She cared nothing for them. Under Rex's protection she could do as she pleased. There was a lot to be said for a husband who was never jealous.

And then something happened that turned her pleasure to unease. Just as the clock struck eleven, the very last moment when new entrants could be admitted, Diantha looked up to see George entering the ballroom.

He didn't see her looking at him. His eyes searched the crowd eagerly until they came to rest on Elinor. As she looked at her cousin's face, and the sudden stillness that had come over her,

Diantha's heart sank. Elinor's eyes blazed with love.

"Countess—" Diantha looked up to find Lord Simon Spenlow regarding her with adoration. He was in his early twenties with a frank, engaging expression and the eager manner of a puppy. "You wore my flowers," he exclaimed breathlessly. "I knew you would—that is—I didn't dare to hope—" He pulled himself together. "May I have the honor of a dance?"

"I'm not sure that that is wise," Diantha began cautiously.

But Lord Simon, emboldened by what he saw as the acceptance of his tribute, seized her card and penciled in his name beside the only dance that hadn't been claimed. It dawned on Diantha that it had been a mistake to wear his roses, but there was nothing to be done about it now. After all, he could hardly make a scene on the dance floor.

In this she was only partly right. Drunk with love and what he thought to be success, Lord Simon poured out his passion into her ears as they circled the floor. Diantha regarded him with fond exasperation. He was so very young, and so madly infatuated with her. It was charming, but it had gone far enough.

"Simon, you're a delightful young man," she said kindly, "but you're much too intense for me. Love is a game, but you won't keep to the rules."

"Don't speak that way," he begged. "Don't try to make me think you're the same as other society women, heartless and cruel, playing with a man for the fun of tormenting him."

"My, my, you have had a full life for one so young!" she teased, trying to defuse the situation with humor. "Come now, you're little more than a schoolboy—"

"No," he interrupted passionately. "I'm a man, madly in love with you. And your heart isn't indifferent. I know it. Oh, if only they hadn't forced you into that cold marriage."

"You know nothing at all about my marriage," Diantha informed him briskly. "I married Chartridge quite willingly."

"How good and generous you are to defend him."

"I'm not good and generous at all," she said with a touch of exasperation. "Chartridge is a delightful husband."

"He married you for your money."

"And I married him for his title, which makes us two of a kind. Do stop talking like a character on the stage, my dear. It just makes me want to laugh."

"You mock me! Cruel woman!"

Despite all her good resolutions, Diantha's lips twitched. Lord Simon saw it. His color rose and the glow of passion in his eyes intensified. She was suddenly aware of her extremely low-cut dress, and wished she could cover herself from his hectic gaze. Luckily the dancing was coming to an end.

"Thank you for a charming dance, Lord Simon," she said primly.

"I shall stay by your side," he declared.

"You'll do no such thing. Do you want to make me the talk of London?"

"Then dance with me again."

"Not for the world. You're too indiscreet, my friend, and this place is very public. Say good night now, and don't speak to me here again."

To her surprise and relief, he obeyed at once, relinquishing her hand to her next partner, and departing with his head high. She went through the steps of a country dance, then joined in the cotillion. When that was over she realized, with a growing sense of disquiet, that she hadn't seen Elinor for some time.

She laughed and flirted as her eyes darted this way and that, and her dread deepened. At last she escaped by pleading a headache, and began to hurry through the anterooms that led off the main ballroom.

In the last one she found Elinor, seated on a low sofa with George, who was holding her hand between both of his. Before either of them saw Diantha, George raised Elinor's hand and pressed it passionately to his lips.

Diantha stood, dismayed, uncertain whether to retreat or advance. While she hesitated, George became aware of her, and sprang to his feet. Diantha hurried into the room and closed the door behind her. "For pity's sake!" she said desperately. "How can you be so reckless?"

"I know what you must think of me," George said, coloring, "but my intentions are honorable. I long to make Elinor my wife, if only—" He relapsed into confusion.

"If only you had enough to live on," Diantha finished sympathetically.

"If I were to sell out," he suggested. "I could find some honorable employment, perhaps in the diplomatic service?"

Elinor and Diantha exchanged looks too fleeting for George to see. He was dear to them both, but even Elinor's love didn't make her think him suitable for the diplomatic service.

"Soldiering is an honorable occupation, and the one to which you are best suited," Diantha said tactfully.

"But the war is over. I can't ask Elinor to live on my pay," George said wretchedly.

"Rex is the head of the family," Diantha mused.

"It would be right and proper for him to make you an allowance."

"He makes me a bachelor's allowance, but I won't take more," George said, going even redder.

She understood him. Any more would have to come from her, and George's pride wouldn't let him accept it.

"Oh, Diantha, help us!" Elinor begged. "We love each other so much. How can we bear it if we can't marry?"

"Of course I'll help you—if I can," Diantha said. "But I don't see what's to be done. My uncle and aunt are the most indulgent parents alive, but you know how they'll regard this match." The two young people looked at each other in despair. "But we won't give up," Diantha said more cheerfully than she felt. "Somehow there must be a way."

She knew that she should make them return to the ballroom with her that instant. Both propriety and good sense demanded it, but some power that she couldn't resist made her say, "I'm going outside now. You can have two minutes. No more. Then Elinor must follow me."

"What shall I do?" George asked trustingly.

Diantha regarded him with fond exasperation. To think he wanted to go into the diplomatic service! "Vanish in another direction," she said, and swept from the room.

Elinor joined her exactly two minutes later, her eyes shining, her hair slightly disarrayed. They returned to the ballroom together, and George didn't appear again that night.

On the way home Elinor sat smiling blissfully. It was clear that her fears had vanished, and she trusted Diantha to think of some brilliant idea. At Gracebourne House, Diantha set her down, and went on her way to her own home, filled with deep foreboding.

In her bedroom she gave herself into Eldon's hands, exhausted by the strain of playing chaperon. She stepped out of her ballgown and into the nightdress that Eldon held up for her. It was a dazzling creation of white lace and silk, cut very low across the bosom, revealing the high, firm swell of her creamy breasts. But what was the point of that, she thought, when Rex wasn't here to admire her?

She put on the matching peignoir, and bid Eldon good night. When she was alone she walked restlessly about the room, unable to settle for the night. If only she could confide her worries to Rex. He could talk to her sensibly and with the familiar humorous gleam in his eyes, and she would know what to do. She knew an unexpected feeling of forlornness. The beautiful room seemed very empty without him.

To distract herself, she considered the three books that lay on her bedside table. As a leader of fashion she must keep abreast of the new novels. There was Sir Walter Scott's *Waverley*, which everyone was talking about. Or *Mansfield Park*, the latest work from the pen of Miss Jane Austen, an author whom Diantha enjoyed for her dry wit. But at last she decided on the third book, Lord Byron's narrative poem *The Corsair*, signed by the author and delivered that very morning. She must be able to converse about it without delay.

After two pages she knew it was going to be hard to get to the end. The hero's aloofness and mystery annoyed her almost as much as Byron himself. Where were the men of good sense—like Rex?

Just when she was trying to decide whether to close the book or suffer longer, Diantha became aware of footsteps running up the stairs. She sat up eagerly. Rex!

But when the door burst open she gave a gasp of horror.

"Lord Simon!"

He was disheveled and slightly flushed, as though with wine. He stood looking at her for a burning moment, then he closed the door behind him and turned the key in the lock.

"How dare you!" Diantha exclaimed. "Leave at once."

He crossed the room in two strides and fell dramatically at her feet. She backed away, clutching the edges of her peignoir together.

"You shall hear me," he said passionately. "I won't leave until I've told you how much I love you—adore you—worship you—"

"Get up, you silly boy," she commanded him. "And leave my room this instant."

She tried to push past him to get to the door, but he clasped his arms around her knees and raised his face imploringly to her. "My love can no longer be silent," he said wildly. "It must speak. It must tell you that you're the most divine woman—no, not a woman, a goddess. Since the moment we met I've been prostrate before you—"

"How very uncomfortable," she observed, trying to turn him aside with humor. But it was useless.

"My heart is yours—"

"But I don't want it," she said, crossly. "Simon dear, you're a very nice boy, but you don't really love me any more than I love you—"

"You mock me!"

"Oh, heavens!" she muttered. "Not you as well!"

"Don't tell me you're indifferent to my passion. You wore my roses, you told me to come to you tonight."

"I did no such thing."

"You said Almack's was too public, and that I must not speak to you *there* again tonight."

"I didn't mean you to come here," she said wildly. "I only meant—oh, I don't know what I meant. I do wish you'd get up."

He did so, but her relief was short-lived. Emboldened by wine and despair, he seized her in his arms and began to plant fierce kisses over her face and neck. Diantha tried to fight him off, but to her horror her struggles caused the peignoir to fall open and slide down, exposing her bosom.

"Let me go," she cried, but Lord Simon was too carried away by his feelings to hear her.

Then came the sound she longed for and dreaded equally. Someone was rattling her door handle from outside, discovering that it was locked. The next moment a boot was put firmly against the door, forcing it open, and there, a whip in his hand, his eyes blazing, stood Rex.

Chapter Six

In an instant Rex took in the scene before him. Then, with an oath, he strode across the room to seize Simon by the scruff of the neck and toss him aside. Diantha sank down onto the bed, hastily covering herself, a prey to relief and mortification equally. She could have screamed with vexation at being found in such a compromising situation by her husband.

"A pretty scene!" he exclaimed. "I return home to hear from my doorman that you shoved past him, barged into my wife's room, and locked the door. What do you have to say for yourself, you young pup?"

Simon scrambled to his feet, no longer the ardent lover, but an awkward boy. But he made a manful effort to rescue his shattered dignity.

"My lord," he said, very red in the face, "there is no excuse for my behavior."

"You needn't tell me that," Rex snapped.

"No excuse but my ardor that—that—" he stammered into silence, under Rex's ironic eye.

"Yes?" Rex encouraged, a glint in his eyes. "Go on, but remember whom you are addressing."

"I've given my heart to Lady Chartridge," Simon declared, "and I'd dared to hope that her heart also—"

"Nonsense!" Rex declared in a voice that was almost amiable. "My wife has no heart. She'd be the first to tell you so."

"That is a foul slander on a wonderful woman!"

"Give me patience!" Rex muttered.

Simon pulled himself together. "I offer you satisfaction, my lord earl."

"Don't talk that theatrical rubbish to me," Rex said, exasperated. "Get out before you feel my boot in your rear."

Simon cast an agonized look at both of them, then fled the room. They heard his feet echoing on the stairs and across the hall, followed by the sound of the front door closing.

Diantha gulped, and braced herself for recriminations. The most tolerant husband alive couldn't overlook a scene like this. But Rex was examining the door that he'd kicked in. It was still on its hinges, although the lock was broken. He closed it carefully, and set a chair beneath the handle, before turning to face her. "Now, madam . . ."

"Rex, I swear I didn't invite that boy here—"

"He thought you did. Really, Diantha, how can you have been so clumsy? A boy of that age doesn't understand that it's all a game. You should confine yourself to fellows who know the rules—like me."

He didn't seem at all angry, and the ironical look was back in his eyes. That was a relief, of course, but she also knew a twinge of disappointment. He ought at least to be offended.

"How can I confine myself to you when you're never here?" she demanded.

"Have I been neglecting you? I thought you did very well without me. Perhaps not quite so well as we both thought. A real woman of the world would never have let matters get to that pass. How did he come to imagine that you had a heart?"

"Because he believes what he wants to believe."

"A common failing to those who are in love," Rex mused. "You wouldn't know that, never having loved. But take my word that it's true."

Diantha stared, arrested by a vibrant note in his voice that she'd never heard before. But before she could speak Rex went on, "You'd better tell me how it happened. How did you meet him? He's new to me."

"He was introduced to me—" She stopped, realizing this might be difficult.

"Where?" Rex demanded inexorably.

"At some social function . . ." she prevaricated.

"Somewhere you had no business to be if your manner tells a true tale. Let me hear the worst."

"It was Bartholomew Fair," she admitted, "and I only went there once, Rex. Aunt Gloria would never allow us to go, and Bertie made it sound so exciting, and I wanted to see the dancing skeleton—"

"And did you see it?" he asked.

"Oh yes, and much more. We all went into the Great Booth to see the theatrical performance *The Horrible Torments of Maria Adley*, and Lord Simon was there and someone introduced us."

"And then?"

"He came up to me at Almack's the following evening, and reminded me that we'd met."

"Showing that he needs a lesson in manners. A man of the world would never have reminded a lady that he'd seen her in such a place."

"I don't think he's very worldly-wise, Rex."

"But *you* pride yourself on being worldly-wise. You should have given him your haughtiest look and told him he was mistaken."

Diantha tried it, looking down her nose and declaiming frostily, "I, sir? In such a place? The idea is absurd."

"Not absurd," Rex corrected her. "Insulting. Always be insulted when you're accused of the truth."

"The idea is insulting," she declaimed, more loftily than ever.

"Excellent," Rex said.

"But he wouldn't have believed me."

"That doesn't matter. He'd have known that he'd overstepped the bounds by speaking of it."

"Oh dear! He seemed such a nice boy that I danced with him. And then he began sending me trinkets—"

"Which you should have returned. But I daresay they got lost among the others."

"Yes," she admitted ruefully. "I mislay the cards, so I don't know who's sent what. So when I see them next I just smile graciously and say how charmed I was with their gift."

Rex's lips twitched. "What a heartless little minx you are," he observed amiably. "The poor devils think their tributes have pleased you, and actually you can't tell one from t'other. So you smiled at this wretched boy, and that was his undoing."

"Oh, I don't think so."

"I do. You haven't seen your own smiles. Calculated to turn a man's insides to water."

"Not calculated," she said quickly. "I just smile without thinking about the effect."

Rex gave an almost inaudible sigh. "How true!" he murmured.

"What was that?"

"Nothing at all. Continue."

"There's not much more to tell. Wherever I went he seemed to be there. I danced with him, told him not to lose his head—"

"But smiling at him while you said it."

"Probably."

"The truth is, you never noticed the poor young pup at all. What made him think otherwise?"

"I happened to mention that I love white roses. He sent me some from the Spenlow hothouses. They were charming, so I wore them tonight."

"Which, of course, he interpreted as encouragement. You should have returned them to him with a freezing note insisting that you preferred orchids."

"They have orchids in the Spenlow hothouses, too," she said in a hollow voice.

"Then tulips, lupines, anything he couldn't get easily. There are tricks to keeping a man on hot coals that you have yet to learn, my clever little witch. So he thought you were giving him a signal and came here tonight—"

"And then I heard him running up the stairs, and he burst into this room. I tried to tell him to go, but he wouldn't listen."

"You must have told him the wrong way."

"I tried to laugh at him—"

"Fatal. To the lover nothing about his love is amusing. You should have been regal, dramatic. *Leave this instant, sir. Or I summon my servants.*"

Diantha drew herself up to her full height and pointed a stern finger at the door. "Leave this instant, sir," she declaimed. "Or I summon my servants."

For answer Rex strode across the room. Before she knew what he meant to do, he'd reached out to her breasts, seized her nightgown, and ripped it from her with one vigorous movement. The delicate material fell to pieces, leaving her completely naked. The next moment she was pulled against him, his arms like steel about her.

"Rex—" she gasped, "you said—"

"I said it would have made *him* leave. Not me."

His lips came down on hers before she could speak. He held her in a ruthless grip, pressing her against the length of his hard body. This was unlike other embraces they'd shared. Suddenly the restrained, gentlemanly lover she'd known was gone. His kiss was fierce, bruising and crushing her mouth as never before.

He moved, turning her in his arms, and she felt herself lifted high against his chest. "*I'm* not a callow boy," he said. "I'm the man you married, and perhaps it's time I reminded you of that fact."

With two steps he reached the bed, tossed her onto it, and began to rip off his clothes. Diantha was suddenly alarmed. She wasn't afraid of Rex, but this was going too fast for her. She put up a hand in protest, but he seized it and pressed it against his mouth, flickering his tongue against the palm in a way that sent fierce tremors of pleasure through her. The sensation was so intense that she gasped wildly and gripped his shoulder with her free hand, digging her nails in.

There was a devilish skill in Rex's tongue. He knew how to make it tease and torment her as he moved over her wrist and along the soft skin of her inner arm, to her elbow, then up to her shoulder. Diantha was caught in the old helpless feeling as the pleasure mounted, mastering her. For once, she wanted to resist it, to talk first, to explain, make Rex understand. But he didn't seem interested in the words she tried to utter, or perhaps he didn't hear them. He reached her shoulders, her neck, and began raining fierce kisses over her breasts. She caught a glimpse of his eyes, and there was something purposeful in them that had never been there before. He was lost in passion, and she had no choice but to lose herself with him.

Her breasts ached for his caresses, the nipples

peaked in proud expectation. He claimed them with tongue and fingers, teasing her to madness. Her efforts to keep control melted in the storm that raged through her. A groan broke from her. It was useless to resist this man who could conquer her with her own pleasure. He pressed her back against the pillows and let one hand wander over her body, caressing her intimately. She felt the light touch of his fingers against her inner thigh, trailing softly upward until he felt the heart of her sensuality, knew that she was ready for him. With one easy movement he was over her, driving into her vigorously. She cried out with pleasure and seized him against her as he thrust again and again.

She'd thought that she knew about the joys of the bed. But the sensations she'd experienced before were tame compared to the whirlwind of pleasure that possessed her now. The excitement mounted to new heights and a sudden wild recklessness came over her. She cried out as her moment came, clinging to Rex, feeling the solid security of his arms about her, catching her as she reached the peak and fell back.

The world would never be the same again. In the riot of sensual delight she'd become a rich, fulfilled woman, whose flesh promised her ever new delights.

Afterward he held her close, murmuring in her ear, "Let your court of gallants know that their days of sighing and swooning are over. I've decided to become a possessive husband—at least until you're a little more skilled in the ways of the world."

"Mmm," she said. Her body was blissfully contented, and she felt no disposition to argue.

She fell asleep at once, and slept against him, without moving, for an hour. She was roused by the feel of his hand between her legs, and awoke to find her body already throbbing with expectation. This time he claimed her at once, entering her slowly and prolonging the moments of pleasure until she was half-crazy. Her climax was explosive, exhausting, and left her in a spin. Looking up, she found him regarding her with a quizzical look. With her senses sharpened, she understood at once. What had just happened was a demonstration of power, reminding her that he was more of a man than any of her courtiers, but most of all reminding her that she belonged to him. He was smiling, but there was a dangerous light behind that smile, and again Diantha realized how little she understood her husband.

"For shame, my lord," she said breathlessly. "Does a gentleman sport with his wife in such a way?"

His smile became a grin, with a hint of cynicism.

"Since this appears to be a night for frankness, then no, mostly not. Such sport is usually saved for a mistress. But as I promised to abandon such pursuits, you'll have to be mistress and wife. Besides, I wanted to know if you'd learned new skills in my absence."

At first she didn't take his meaning. Then a surge of anger made her struggle, but he held her tight, not fighting her, but waiting for her to recognize the futility of fighting him. "How dare you say such a thing," she raged, beating him with her fists. "It's an insult."

"But you've been at such pains to appear a woman of the world," he reminded her.

"But to suggest that I would—before I've even given you an heir." The dreadful words were out before she could stop them, and the next moment she wanted to die of mortification. How could she have said such a thing?

But instead of being angry, Rex gave a crack of laughter. His arms tightened about her as his powerful body shook.

"You've learned more than I thought," he said at last.

"Rex—I didn't mean—you can't think that—"

"Hush, I know what to think of you, my infuriating treasure. What that poor boy believed he was doing falling in love with you, I can't imagine. What a bore you must have found him!"

"A dead bore," she said with relief. "You know my views of love."

"Views that I share. But besides, love, there is also pleasure, which neither of us finds a bore."

As he spoke he ran a finger lightly down over her breasts. In an instant desire awoke in her again, and she craved him as urgently as if the last half hour had never been. He sensed her eager response and drew her against him. "You have still much to learn about pleasure," he murmured. "And I love to teach. . . . Now, my heartless minx . . ."

"I came as soon as I received Lady Gracebourne's message," Diantha said, hurrying in.

Ferring, the butler who'd been with the Gracebournes as long as she could remember, and knew all their secrets, lowered his voice.

"Such a to-do, there's been, your ladyship," he said worriedly. "There's my lady prostrate with the vapors, and Lady Elinor in tears, and his lordship locked in his study, sunk in gloom."

"Good heavens! Whatever has happened?"

"All I know is that it has something to do with Major Lytham."

"Diantha!"

She looked up to see Elinor peering over the rail at her. Even at this distance Diantha could see that Elinor's face was distraught.

"Don't disturb Lady Gracebourne just yet," she told Ferring. "I'll talk to Lady Elinor first."

She hurried up to her cousin's bedroom and as soon as she was inside Elinor locked the door behind them. She was pale and looked as though she'd been crying, but there was also a touch of defiance in her normally gentle face.

"Tell me what's happened," Diantha said, throwing off her cloak and taking Elinor's hands between hers. "Is it George?"

Elinor nodded. "He's written to Papa, asking to see him tomorrow. He—he means to ask for my hand. Papa understood that, of course, and asked me if I'd encouraged him. I said I had, that I loved him and wanted to marry him. And—Papa said—" Elinor's voice wobbled.

"The match doesn't please him?" Diantha asked gently. She drew Elinor to sit on the bed.

"He says he'll see George out of courtesy, but he'll never sanction our marriage. He says George hasn't a penny of his own—"

"That is unfortunately true," Diantha murmured.

"As though I cared," Elinor cried passionately. "George and I have thought it all out. We know it must be a long engagement, before he's in a position to marry. And I'll wait for him gladly. But Papa said I can never marry him and—oh, Diantha, I love him so much. How can I bear it if they part us?"

She flung herself facedown, sobbing as if her heart would break. Diantha tried to soothe her, but Elinor's grief mounted, and when she tried to speak again the words were muffled.

"What did you say, my darling?" Diantha asked.

"Papa wants me to marry Sir Cedric Delamere," Elinor choked. "I'd rather die."

Diantha considered Sir Cedric. He was wealthy and kind, but he was also middle-aged, plain, and much given to sober reflection. No girl who'd formed a lasting passion for a major of dragoons would look twice at Sir Cedric.

"What am I going to do?" Elinor sobbed.

Diantha stiffened her chin in sudden resolution. "You're going to dry your eyes, and don't fall into a despair," she said firmly. "There is always a solution."

"For you, yes. You're so strong, and determined. But nothing can save George and me but a—a fairy godmother."

Diantha's lips twitched. "Well, who knows? Fairy godmothers come in all shapes and sizes," she said lightly.

She went next to her aunt's room, and found her lying on her bed, with the shades down, dabbing her brow with lavender water.

"Thank heavens you're here," she said tearfully. "I declare I don't know what I'm doing. It's all so dreadful."

"Not dreadful at all, dear Aunt," Diantha said cheerfully, pulling the curtains back. Lady Gracebourne covered her eyes. "I promise you, there's nothing to fall into gloom about."

"Nothing to—? Here's Elinor declaring she'll marry a penniless—of course, I know he's your brother-in-law and his lineage is impeccable, but what use is a title in the family if it's never going to be his?"

Diantha chuckled. "Very true. And I'm such a contrary creature that I'm bound to give Chartridge an heir just to cut poor George out."

Lady Gracebourne gave a little scream. "Oh, good

heavens! I didn't mean—you can't think—how can you say such a terrible thing?"

Diantha laughed again. "Dear Aunt, don't put yourself into a pucker. You know it's my way to say outrageous things."

"Diantha, what am I to do? I'm *not* a heartless parent—"

"Of course you're not. Nobody knows your kindness better than I."

Lady Gracebourne raised a tearful face to her. "And I'd never force my child into a distasteful marriage—"

"Uncle Selwyn seems very set on Sir Cedric Delamere, but he won't do, you know."

"He didn't mean what he said. He wasn't himself. Tomorrow he'll receive George with all kindness and explain why it isn't possible. Although I must say I'm surprised at George fixing Elinor's interest before he'd spoken to her papa."

"I don't suppose people think of things like that when they're in love," Diantha mused. "But before Uncle Selwyn rejects George, I think he should hear about his property."

Lady Gracebourne struggled up in bed. "Property? What property?"

"George isn't penniless at all," Diantha said gaily. "To be sure, he isn't rich, but he has a respectable little property and can support Elinor in comfort."

"But why didn't we hear of this before? Why didn't Elinor tell us?"

"It's happened very recently," Diantha said, improvising quickly. "George was left an estate by a distant uncle. It's not as large as Sir Cedric's, of course, but it will be enough for him to marry."

Unkind persons had been known to call Lady Gracebourne as brainless as a chicken, but she had a certain shrewdness where people were concerned.

She straightened her cap and regarded Diantha suspiciously. "What is the name of this distant uncle?" she demanded.

"For the moment I cannot recall it," Diantha said with perfect truth.

Their eyes met for a long, silent moment. "Will it do?" Lady Gracebourne asked at last.

"I'm sure it will. Leave it to me, dear Aunt."

Diantha kissed her briefly, charged her to tell Elinor that all would soon be well, and hurried away. On the way home her mind seethed with plans. Luckily she saw George as soon as she was inside the door, forbade him to visit the Gracebournes without speaking with her first, and hurried into Rex's study. To her relief, he was there.

"Whatever is the matter?" he asked, eyeing her agitation in some amusement.

"Rex, I need your help. I've been telling the most terrible lies, and you must help me to back them up."

He grinned. "If this is another of your admirers—"

"No, no, that's all finished. This is much more important. It's about George and Elinor."

Rex sighed. "He's been talking to me. He plans to sell out of the army and seek employment, but I can't think that will be enough to satisfy the Gracebournes."

"I've just come from there, and the house is in uproar. Elinor is distraught, and I simply can't have her made unhappy. Something must be done."

"Hence the tall stories?" Rex asked satirically.

"Terrible ones. They must be made true immediately. Do you remember Ainsley Court, which Mr. Ainsley was trying to sell to pay his gambling debts?"

"Indeed I do."

"It would suit George and Elinor perfectly, especially as it's so near to us. If it's brought into order, the rents will provide a respectable income, and if you continue George's allowance, I don't see why they shouldn't—"

"Wait," Rex interrupted. "George doesn't own Ainsley Court."

"But he will when we've bought it. I've told my aunt that George has recently come into a property, and Ainsley Court will do perfectly."

Rex frowned. "It won't do at all," he said shortly.

"But I've told them now. Oh, Rex, I know I should have spoken to you first, but it all came out in a burst of inspiration. You *can't* tell them I was making it up."

"No need for that. We need only say you misunderstood. I inherited some money from my father. It isn't much—" his mouth twisted wryly "—compared to the Halstow fortune. But it kept me in modest comfort before our marriage. I intend to pass it over to George. He doesn't have expensive habits and should be able to support a wife on it."

"But you mustn't do that," Diantha burst out, horrified.

A sudden chill came over Rex's face, like a visor, shutting her out. "Indeed, my dear, I can think of no reason why I shouldn't. It's for me to maintain my brother, not you."

She flinched at his tone, and cursed her own clumsiness. To have spoken to the Gracebournes before Rex was tactless, and would make her husband feel she was using her wealth to ride roughshod over him, the very thing that most angered him. She knew her fears were right when Rex tried to turn away from her, back to his desk.

Diantha felt suddenly desperate. So far they'd

managed their marriage lightheartedly, shying away from those subjects that would reveal that their minds were out of tune. But they couldn't live their whole lives like that. A wrong move now might mean they never understood each other. She darted forward and dropped onto a footstool beside him, taking his arms and forcing him to look at her.

"Listen to me, Rex," she said urgently. "Whatever happens, you mustn't give away your own fortune. I know how much you value it, and I know why. Because it makes you independent of me. If you lose it, you'll have nothing but what comes from me, and you'll hate that. And very soon—" for some reason she found her voice shaking "—very soon—you would come to hate me. I know you would. And you know it, too, don't you?"

He colored uncomfortably. "Nonsense, my dear."

"It isn't nonsense. This has always been between us. Sometimes I think you've come close to hating me already—"

"No, no—" he said hastily.

"You can't deny that it's an uncomfortable position for you."

"Sometimes," he confessed with a grimace, "but I had hoped that I'd hidden it better than that."

"And it'll get worse if you have nothing of your own. Won't it?" She waited for him to reply, but he was silent. Diantha had a terrible sensation of floundering and not knowing how to help herself. She knew a little of how Rex felt, but she also knew that there were dark depths to which she was never admitted. She tightened her hold on his arms, shaking him a little. "Please, Rex. Don't refuse me this."

"Is it supposed to make me feel less dependent to have you support my brother?" he asked at last in a cool voice.

"I'm doing it for Elinor," she said at once. "Well, a little for George, too, because I'm so very fond of him. But think of this as Elinor's dowry. She's like my sister. If I choose to do something for her, surely that's up to me? But most of all, you must not—*must* not—give up your independence. Surely you understand why?"

"Yes, I do," he replied gently. "But until this moment, I didn't know that *you* did."

She colored. "I'm not as stupid as you think me," she said.

"I never thought you stupid, Diantha." He stroked her cheek. "Perhaps a little blinkered, now and then. But not today."

"I do understand you sometimes, don't I?" she asked with a touch of eagerness that made him smile.

"A woman of superior understanding," he agreed. "Very well. You'd better tell me exactly what you want me to do."

"Oh, no," she said hastily. "I leave the management of the affair to you."

He cocked an eyebrow at her. "Afraid of being thought a managing female, Diantha? Come, this meekness doesn't suit you."

"Well, I'm doing my best," she said with an indignation that made him grin.

"This is your campaign," he said. "You arrange matters with Delaney."

She sighed with pleasure. "At least we saved George from the diplomatic service. Or do I mean saved the diplomatic service from George?"

"The diplomatic service?" he echoed. "Whoever made such a ridiculous suggestion?"

"He did. It's his idea of employment."

"Good God, the country would be at war again in days!"

Their eyes met. At the same moment they burst into laughter. He leaned down and kissed her.

"I'm so glad we've found a way," she said. "They love each other terribly. It would have broken their hearts if they couldn't marry."

He raised an eyebrow. "My dear, I do believe you're turning into a romantic."

"No such thing!" she said hotly. "How dare you insult me so, my lord!"

"There!" he said appreciatively. "Just as I taught you! Always be insulted when accused of the truth."

"But it isn't the truth!"

"Your pardon, my lady. Your concern for two people in the toils of love misled me. So against your principles."

"Oh, what do principles matter where people are concerned?" she demanded.

"Spoken like a true woman." His eyes were still alight with laughter. "Perhaps we should call George in and coach him for his part."

For George's sake they smudged the details of the plan. This was easy to do since he had no idea how little money had passed directly to Rex on his marriage. He emerged from the interview with the vague idea that Ainsley Court would be Rex's gift, which was exactly what Diantha had intended.

It was a day or two before Lord and Lady Gracebourne were won over. They would have preferred a grand match for their daughter, but they were fond parents, and once assured of her future comfort, they were unable to hold out longer against her passionate entreaties. Delaney was dispatched to purchase Ainsley Court, and by the end of the week everything was settled. George was to sell out of the army, and the marriage would take place as soon as possible. The young couple would spend their honeymoon in their new home, and in

December would join Rex and Diantha at Chartridge Abbey.

Elinor's wedding day dawned in the gray mists of November, but nobody heeded that. Light and happiness filled the house as she dressed in her bridal gown, assisted by her mother and Diantha. When at last she stood arrayed in white satin and lace, she turned to her cousin, her eyes shining.

"Oh, Diantha," she breathed. "I owe it all to you. Mama told me how you did everything. My dearest cousin, how can I ever thank you?"

"By being happy," Diantha said, laughing as she received Elinor's hug.

"I *am* happy. How could I be anything else, with my darling George? I love him so much."

"I'm afraid you do, my poor dear," Diantha mocked lightly. "Ah, if only I'd had my way. I'd have saved you from such a misfortune, and chosen a rational match for you, like mine."

"Like yours?" Elinor stared at her.

"To be sure. Rex and I deal very well together. I can recommend a marriage based on good sense, but perhaps it wouldn't suit everyone." She kissed Elinor and said, "I must go down and have a word with Uncle Selwyn."

"Why, what is it, my love?" Lady Gracebourne asked when Diantha had gone. "You look so strange."

"It's Diantha, Mama. Sometimes she's so very, very clever. And sometimes—she's not clever at all."

"Very true," Lady Gracebourne said, nodding sagely. "But we must leave her to discover that for herself. Now, if you are ready . . ."

The wedding was held at St. George's, Hanover Square. Elinor looked a vision as she walked down the aisle on her father's arm, her face glowing with joy as she came to stand beside George. He was pale and nervous, and Rex, his groomsman, put a reassuring hand on his shoulder.

As they exchanged vows Diantha sent up a silent prayer that this love match might not go the way of others. She thought of Lord Farrell, so madly in love with Charlotte when they married, so soon grown careless. And Charlotte, who'd once adored her husband, now contemptuous of him, with only her children for comfort.

And before them, her own mother and father, a passionate elopement ending in bitterness and dislike. That was what became of love. Only, let it be different for Elinor and George, she prayed.

She thought of her own marriage, wherein there could be no disillusion, because there had been no illusions. She was safe and contented. But when she saw the radiance on Elinor's face as George slipped the ring onto her finger, Diantha knew a little pang. She'd made her choice, and was satisfied with it. There would be no troughs of despair for her. But no peaks of glory either.

Glancing up, she saw Rex's eyes on her, and wondered if he could read her thoughts. What was going through his own head? Did he have any regrets about his bargain? She colored and looked away from him.

Afterward there was merrymaking in Gracebourne House. The tables and sideboards groaned under the weight of jellies, creams, and ices. The wedding cake was five tiers high. Diantha found herself talking to distant relations she'd never known she possessed.

"You look very like your mother," a thin, elderly woman told her. "She was darker, but you have her face."

"You—knew my mother, ma'am?"

"I'm your great-aunt Helena. Alva was my niece, almost a daughter to me. Such a sweet creature, but headstrong. Very headstrong. I warned her how it would be with that scoundrel she married, but once she'd got the bit between her teeth, she'd never listen."

"By 'scoundrel' I assume you mean my father?" Diantha asked coolly.

"Who else should I mean?" the old woman demanded sharply. She seemed to feel that her age gave her the privilege of rudeness, for she went on, "He was a bad lot, through and through. No woman of taste should have looked at him, but he cast a spell over my poor Alva."

To Diantha's relief, Rex appeared at her elbow. Great-Aunt Helena barely waited for the introductions before plunging on, "I must congratulate you on rising above him. Done very well for yourself, haven't you? The Halstow money, of course. You can thank your luck your father died before he got his hands on it, or there would have been precious little left for you."

Here Rex intervened firmly, contriving to silence the old woman with such tact that it was only later she fully realized that she'd been snubbed. By then Rex had drawn Diantha away.

"The bride and groom are about to leave," he told her.

The chaise was at the door. Elinor threw her arms around her parents, and then Diantha, while George, by now beyond speech, shook Rex's hand vigorously. Then they were running down the stairs, climbing into the chaise, and they were away. Diantha watched them go, with a little ache in her heart. She wasn't sure why.

"Can we go home now, Rex?"

"You, certainly. But I'm engaged with a party of friends. I did mention it."

"Oh yes, so you did," she said hastily.

"Would you prefer that I cancel it?"

She longed to say yes, but remembering their agreement to live independently, she stifled the wish and smiled brightly. "Certainly not. I shall attend the opera. I'll return home now, to change my attire."

Chapter Seven

But when Diantha was at home all desire to go to the opera left her. Her head hurt, and after a light supper she retired to her room. She tried to read, but found she couldn't concentrate. Visions of Elinor and George, their faces alight with happiness, danced before her. She wondered if they, too, would discover the physical delights of marriage. And it came to her, with a sudden pain, that for them there would be no turning away from each other in the morning. They would sleep, arms entwined, and awaken still embracing. In the daylight they would smile at each other with eyes full of the memory of the night. Not like her and Rex.

If only he would return and take her in his arms. Then, in the heat of their bed, they would enjoy the sensuality that briefly united them. And she would try again to believe that it was enough.

She went to her dressing table and pulled out the bottom drawer, sliding her hand deep inside until her fingertips found a concealed spring. A touch and another drawer slid open inside the first. It was a hiding place where a woman might conceal letters from a secret lover. But the letters Diantha kept there were from her father, plus a miniature, showing him as a young man.

She was ambivalent about her father. She knew he'd treated her mother badly, because Alva had lost no chance to say so. But in his careless way he'd been fond of his daughter, always bringing her pretty presents on his visits home, and making her laugh with his outrageous stories. And he'd written to her, witty, affectionate letters that she treasured still.

The picture had come to her only recently, with her grandfather's estate. She studied it now, with softened eyes. It had been painted when Blair was a young man, before dissipation had coarsened his features, but it was sufficiently like the man she remembered to bring an ache to her heart.

She settled herself comfortably on the carpet beside the dressing table and began to read the letters again. The remembered warmth of his affection made her feel less lonely, and a little smile touched her lips. Absorbed as she was, she didn't notice the passage of time, until something in the silence made her look up to find Rex standing there, watching her with a curious look on his face.

He was still dressed, but in his shirtsleeves, his ruffled shirt open at the throat. He put out a hand to help her to her feet, saying coolly, "Concealed drawers, clandestine correspondence! Fie, Diantha! How vulgar!"

His words were clear, yet she had the impression that he'd drunk more than usual tonight. Normally Rex drank sparingly, saying that too much alcohol ruined a man's sporting performance, but now there was something different in his manner, and his eyes were brilliant.

"You're quite out, my lord," she said. "I have no secret admirer. In fact, I have no admirer of any kind since you sent them packing. These letters are from my father."

To her amazement his mouth twisted violently in

an expression of cruel cynicism. "It's true," she insisted. "He sent them to me years ago, in the last months before his death. I've kept them because—well, they're all I have of him. Those and his picture."

She placed the miniature before him, and as he stared at it a terrible stillness came over him. In the candlelight it was hard to read his exact expression, but there was no mistaking the tension that radiated from his whole body. "Yes," he murmured, his eyes fixed on the picture of Blair Halstow. "Yes."

"Did you—did you know him?" she asked.

"I never exchanged so much as one word with your father," Rex said in a deliberate voice that struck oddly on her ear.

"I see," she faltered. "I just thought—I know so little about him—except what my mother told me. She used to blackguard him, just as that woman did tonight. I hated it."

"Your mother criticized your father to you? She shouldn't have done so, however bad he was."

"Why do you say he was bad?" Diantha demanded quickly. "You didn't know him." Her voice rose on a note of anger. "You know nothing about him."

Rex drew a breath. "Of course not. But I hear only bad things of him. Even his own wife seems to have spoken ill of him to his child—"

"He was kind to me," Diantha said with a touch of wistfulness. "I knew him very little, but he used to send me presents. And letters. I didn't get them at first. Mama tore them up. Then he came home and found out, and there was the most frightful quarrel. After that, Mama let me have them, but always with pursed lips and sighs of disapproval.

She got very angry when I wouldn't let her read them, but they were just between him and me."

"And you keep them still," Rex said in a brooding voice. "Locked away like treasures. How sentimental. How unwise!"

"He wasn't as bad as people said, Rex. I know he wasn't. When he was at home he often had more time for me than Mama. He used to ask me what I'd been learning, and make me show him my sketches, and—and dance with me—" She choked suddenly, for a wave of memory had washed over her. Rex watched her, his face harsh, like a man in pain.

"After he died," she went on after a moment, "Mama often said that he'd cared nothing for either of us. But she said that because she hated him. She'd have said anything. I often think that if Papa hadn't died when he did, we might have grown to be even closer."

He gave a curt laugh. "I'm surprised at you, Diantha. I thought you had too much good sense to put any man on a pedestal."

"But this is my father," she protested. "I don't see him in the same light as other men."

"And you're wrong. He *was* a man as other men, and your mother knew it. Remember I once said to you, 'What woman could respect her husband if she knew half his activities?' Your mother did know. That's why she spoke of him as she did."

"But she would never speak of the way he died," Diantha said. "And I think I know why. I think he was ill and alone. Perhaps he was asking for her—for me—and she wouldn't let me go."

"Nonsense!"

She looked up, amazed by the bitterness in Rex's voice. The harsh look on his face deepened, and there was a cold glitter in his eyes that she'd seen once before: the first evening, when they'd danced and he said his experience of women had been "damnable."

"You know nothing about it," he said sharply. "This is a pretty dream that you've created about a man who's safely dead. If you're going to idealize a man, it's always better if he's dead. Then you don't risk the disillusion of reality."

The injustice of this stung her to retort, "How do you know that it would have been disillusion?"

"He was a man, wasn't he?" Rex flung at her. "A lying, cheating rogue, who cared nothing for whom he hurt so long as he had his pleasures—"

"You said you didn't know him—"

He drew a swift breath. "I said he was a man as other men. All men are like that."

"Not you," she said swiftly.

"What do you know of me? Do you think I'm any better than the others? Do you think I can't be cruel and unforgiving—?"

At that moment she could have believed anything of him. In the candlelight his face was almost satanic. "You're right," she said slowly. "I know nothing about you."

"Except the wrong that I did you."

"What wrong did you ever do me?"

"To marry you. To let you sleepwalk into a marriage with a man you don't love, for my own benefit. Oh yes, *I've* gained from it, but what have you gained, except a desert?"

"But—we talked about that—"

"Oh yes, we talked. A man in his thirties, who'd lived a man's life, who'd known the heights and the depths, talked with a girl of twenty who'd seen nothing and done nothing. He could see that she didn't know what she was talking about, but he let her go on, because it suited him. He let her believe she could live without love, when he knew different. He knew that one day she'd fall in love, and when that day came she'd hate him. And if he'd had a shred of decency, he'd have turned away from her. But he was a selfish rogue, so he let her walk into disaster with a smile on her face."

"Our marriage—a disaster?"

"For you—yes."

"But, Rex—truly you're wrong. If you're thinking of my flirtations, they meant nothing. I never loved any of them, not for a minute."

He gave her a twisted smile. "I wasn't thinking of them, Diantha. I know full well you never loved them."

"I've no reason to hate you. You said yourself that I have no heart, and—and I think you were right. I haven't fallen in love with anyone—"

He came closer and stood looking down at her. "Are you quite sure of that?" he asked softly.

She could feel the heat from his body. It made her dizzy and she had to fight to speak calmly. "Truly, there's no one. I don't think there ever could be. I just seem to be armored." She gave an unconscious sigh. "Perhaps I'm just different from the rest of my sex."

"Not all," he said slowly. "I knew another woman once who couldn't love—but she wasn't like you. Her eyes didn't open wide in that trusting way you have, and she never laughed: not really laughed as you do. Her laugh was cold and brittle, and calculated to wound—"

Diantha grew very still. Rex spoke as though he could see beyond her to some tormenting vision. He put both hands at the sides of her head and searched her face from dark, hooded eyes.

"And yet you are her sister, after all," he murmured. "A heart protected with armor, unyielding—what do you know of the torments of mere mortals? Can a kiss warm you to life?"

He pulled her to him suddenly, and crushed his mouth to hers. No kiss he'd given her before had ever been like this. There was none of the tenderness she was used to, and even the passion was flavored by something else. Bitterness, anger, perhaps even hate: she could sense these in the steel grip of his arms, the fierce caresses of his lips.

He kissed her mouth, her neck, her breasts, murmuring hot, incoherent words.

"Rex," she gasped. "Please—no—"

He looked down at her from blazing eyes, and she had the unnerving sensation that he didn't see her at all. There was someone else in his arms, someone who brought a look of hell to his face: a woman who'd touched his heart as his wife never could.

"A chaste wife," he murmured, "caring nothing for those she tortures. Mocking them. Laughing at them with her—" A shudder went through his powerful frame. "What do you care? What did she care?"

"She?" Diantha breathed. "Who?"

"Who?" He seemed to come out of a dream. Diantha could see the shock in his eyes. "Why—no one." He stepped back sharply as though the touch of her burned him. His chest rose and fell under the influence of some massive emotion.

"Rex—" She reached out to him, but he moved away.

"Keep away from me," he said savagely. "I shouldn't have come here—I should never—"

Without another word he turned and left the room. A second later Diantha heard the key being turned in the lock of their connecting door.

She lay awake until dawn, thinking of this new

side to Rex that she'd seen tonight. It had startled her, yet at the same time she felt she'd gained an intriguing glimpse into his real self. She wanted to know more.

She rose early next morning to make sure of seeing him in case he went out early. When he came into the breakfast room in riding dress and started on seeing her, she knew she'd been right. He'd wanted to avoid her.

"It's unlike you to be so early," he observed coolly. "However, it gives me a chance to apologize for my behavior of last night."

"There's no need—"

"But there is. I'd had, as you must have guessed, a large amount of brandy. It was unforgivable of me to appear before you in such a state. Perhaps you will be kind enough to overlook it, and forget everything that happened."

"I don't want to forget it," she said stubbornly.

"You wish to reproach me? Well, I don't deny I deserve it."

"I don't want to reproach you, just to talk to you. Last night—"

"Last night I said and did a great many things that meant nothing; things I would prefer to forget." He looked at her with wintry eyes. *"Things that do not concern my wife."*

Before that deliberate snub she could do nothing but retreat. He saw her go pale and a faint smile touched his countenance.

"Come, my dear, you and I have managed to live peaceably by keeping our distance. Let us continue in this way, and show the world the picture of an amiable marriage."

"If that is what you prefer," she said in a colorless voice.

Rex raised her hand to his lips.

"I'll leave you now. I'm sure you are deep in preparations for our departure and will be wishing me out of your way."

It was the reverse of what she wished, but she didn't dare say so for fear of another snub. She watched dumbly as Rex walked out.

But there was little time for her to brood. It would soon be her first Christmas as Lady Chartridge, and there were a thousand plans to be made. A week later the house was shut up and they were on their way to the country.

Christmas at Chartridge Abbey bid fair to be the merriest there for years, so Lopping confided to Diantha in a rare moment of condescension, and the demeanor of the other servants confirmed it. Elinor and George joined them in December, and one glance was enough to show Diantha that they were ecstatically happy. In a few short weeks Elinor had blossomed from a shy girl into a poised young woman, confident of her husband's love and her place in the world. As for George, whenever he thought himself unobserved, he followed his wife with his eyes.

Like Diantha, Elinor conceived an immediate liking for Sophie, and the three young women plunged happily into planning the tenants' party.

"There hasn't been one since I can remember," Sophie told them excitedly. "The last earl—" She checked herself and blushed.

"Was too mean," Diantha finished for her, with a chuckle. "I do hope you'll come to all the parties, Sophie."

"I'll try, thank you. But Christmas is such a busy time for Papa that naturally I must do as he wishes. And there'll be my aunt Felicia to be attended to. She is to pay us an extended visit, with one of her nieces."

Hearing a little constraint in Sophie's voice Diantha demanded instant enlightenment. It appeared that the niece, Miss Amelia Dawlish, was young and headstrong, and had been placed in the charge of her strict aunt in order to prevent her from damaging herself before she was old enough to appear in society.

"I gather that she's a great beauty, and her parents hope to marry her well, in a worldly sense," Sophie said. "So she is to spend Christmas with us and Aunt Felicia in the hope that Papa may prove a beneficial influence."

Diantha's first sight of the beauty came three days later at church, and she almost forgot her manners and stared, for although only sixteen, Amelia was already startlingly lovely. But it soon appeared that her behavior was hoydenish, almost to the point of vulgarity. She looked around the church, smiled saucily at the young men, and whispered to her aunt during the sermon, despite being repeatedly hushed. When presentations were made later she greeted Lord and Lady Chartridge boldly.

"I swear I was ready to die if the sermon had lasted much longer," she said with a giggle. "Lord, I don't know how people endure it."

"To say such a thing with Sophie standing there!" Diantha exclaimed on the way home. "I think she must be a saint to preserve her temper. And the worst of it is, we shall be obliged to invite Amelia with the others."

Receiving no answer from Elinor, she looked across and saw her cousin smiling at her new husband, and trying to disguise the fact that they were holding hands in Elinor's muff. Perceiving her eyes upon them, they pulled apart self-consciously.

"And you married for all of a month," she teased them. "I don't know what the world is coming to."

Rex grinned. "Not everyone has your strong mind and devotion to Reason, my dear," he said.

He spoke in his old way, with cheerful amusement, and no hint of an undercurrent. The night when he'd let his mask slip might never have been. It left Diantha bewildered and almost wondering if she'd imagined the things he'd said, the look she'd seen in his eyes.

The vicar and his family came to dine the following week, and Diantha's pity for Sophie deepened. Not only was Amelia unpleasantly bold, but Aunt Felicia had an elevated idea of her own consequence. She was as conscious of her noble relations as the vicar and Sophie were indifferent to them, and made continual references to "my kinsman, Viscount Ellesmere." She had visited his country seat once, long ago, and now lived on the memory.

At last dinner was over, the gentlemen had joined the ladies in the drawing room, and the tea tray arrived. The conversation turned to the tenants' party, which prompted Aunt Felicia to hold forth on the customs at Ellesmere Park. Just as Diantha was wondering how she could stem the flow she heard the sound of wheels on the carriageway outside.

"Who can be arriving at this hour?" she wondered. "Good heavens! That sounds like Bertie's voice."

The next moment Lopping entered and murmured, "The Honorable Mr. Bertram Foxe begs a word with you in private, my lady."

Filled with curiosity, Diantha hurried into the hall, where she discovered Bertie, splendidly attired in a drab driving coat with a dozen capes, looking agitated. "Glad to find you at home," he said. "The fact is—know I wasn't invited and all that—"

"You would have been, if I hadn't known that you despised the country," she told him, smiling.

"Ah, well—may have decided too hastily. Much to be said for rustic pursuits, especially at Christmas," he said, with an attempt at a hearty laugh.

Asking no further questions, Diantha gave instructions for the stabling of Bertie's horses, then summoned her housekeeper and ordered a room prepared. Bertie's valet went to unpack his gear.

"Come and join us," Diantha invited, indicating the drawing room, from where the sound of Amelia's laughter could be heard.

"Er—not fit to appear before ladies," he demurred, indicating his travel-stained appearance.

But the next moment Amelia's head appeared around the door. Her eyes brightened with pleasure at the sight of one who was clearly a dandy, and the next moment she danced out, demanding to be introduced.

Diantha gave a silent groan at this forward behavior, but Bertie seemed untroubled by it. His eyes were riveted on Amelia's lovely face, and he stammered out a few words without seeming to know what he said.

To Diantha's relief Sophia came quickly after Amelia, gently restraining her volatile cousin. Diantha made hasty introductions, after which there was nothing for it but to take Bertie into the drawing room. Aunt Felicia was condescendingly gracious, and the vicar greeted him with quiet courtesy, though he looked gravely at Bertie's dapper-dog appearance. Before long he announced that it was time for them to depart. Amelia pouted, but he was insistent, and the vicarage party departed. Soon after that George and Elinor retired for the night, leaving Bertie alone with Rex and Diantha.

Bertie cast an awkward glance at Rex, feeling the air heavy with memories of their first encounter. Rex had bought back the horse by sending his man to see Bertie, so apart from a brief greeting at the wedding, this was the first time they'd met since the day in the park. But he was relieved to notice that Chartridge seemed in good humor, and Rex's first words confirmed it. "You're welcome here, of course," he declared, "but what brings you out to the country in midwinter? These surely aren't your natural haunts?"

"No knowing when a fellow may change his habits," Bertie said gamely. "Got a notion to spend Christmas quietly."

"No, no," Rex reproved him. "That story will do for others, not for us. What is it? Debts?"

Bertie made a last attempt to stand on his dignity. "Why should you think of that? I don't know what Diantha's been telling you—"

"Nonsense, of course you do," Rex said with a grin. "Are you sure it isn't debts?"

"No such thing. Got no debts to speak of. At least, no more than usual."

"How much?" Diantha asked, amused.

"I wish you wouldn't be harping on about money when a fellow's in trouble," Bertie said irritably.

"I'm sorry, Bertie dear, but 'trouble' with you has always meant money."

"Not this time, apparently," Rex murmured. "Besides, Diantha, didn't you hear him say that he didn't mean to hang upon your purse strings? A comforting reflection for you."

Bertie, who hadn't precisely said this, gulped, but, meeting Rex's eyes, subsided. Lopping arrived at that moment with refreshments, and Bertie had a few merciful minutes to collect himself. It was difficult when his host was regarding him with a satirical gleam, but he tried.

"If it isn't money, what is it?" Diantha asked. "I'm at one with Chartridge in being unconvinced by this sudden taste for rustic life. So far from London! Whoever would have thought it?"

"No one," Bertie said. "That's just it. No one will think of looking—er—that is—forgot what I was going to say."

"Are you perhaps on the run?" Rex asked sympathetically. "Not, I trust, from the law."

"Certainly not!" Bertie said, shocked. "Never been in trouble with the law. Never even boxed the watch."

"My dear fellow, I do beg your pardon. Then I'm at a standstill."

"Ain't suitable for a female's ears," Bertie murmured, with a harassed glance at his cousin.

"A high flyer," Diantha exclaimed, entranced.

"Eh?" Bertie sat up straight.

"Not high flyer? Prime article? Rex, help me."

"You're doing excellently well, m'dear. Lightskirt. Piece of virtue. They all mean the same."

"But *she* shouldn't know anything about it," her cousin yelped. "Chartridge, you really shouldn't let her talk like that."

"My wife doesn't apply to me for permission for anything she chooses to say," Rex said with a grin. "You may speak freely before her."

"Well, I don't know about—" he mumbled.

"Bertie, if you don't tell me this instant what sent you hurrying down here seeking our protection, I shall turn you out into the snow," Diantha threatened.

"It ain't snowing," he protested blankly.

"Then I shall turn you out into whatever it *is*

doing," she declared, exasperated beyond endurance.

Bertie wasn't skilled with words, so the story came out haltingly. It appeared that he'd recently met a young widow called Mrs. Templeton, and there had sprung up between them a pure and virtuous love, which, for reasons left vague, had not resulted in marriage.

"Go on," Diantha commanded, much entertained by Bertie's frantic efforts to edit the story for her ears.

"Well—then her husband showed up."

Diantha frowned. "I thought she was a widow."

"*I* thought she was a widow," Bertie yelped. "That's what she said. But no such thing, apparently. And this fellow says—well, compromised, you know—wants satisfaction. And I don't know what I've said to send you into whoops."

With a supreme effort Lord and Lady Chartridge brought themselves under control, wiping their eyes. "I'm sorry, Bertie," Diantha said in a choking voice. "But the thought of you—in a duel—" She went off into another peal of laughter while her wretched victim fulminated in silence. A glance at Rex's face revealed that the earl was as devoid of proper feeling as his wife.

"So you ran away," Rex said with a grin. "Very wise."

"I didn't run away," Bertie said with a last attempt at dignity. "It ain't running away to—I mean, lady's reputation and all that. And besides—you don't think they'll look here, do you?"

"If they do, you may be sure we'll protect you," Diantha assured him. "But I wonder how you'll enjoy country life. We live very simply, you know. Early to bed, early to rise, dinner at six, plenty of energetic pursuits, and strict attendance at church."

"That sounds splendid," Bertie declared heroically. "Just what I—er—suit me down to the ground."

"Have some brandy," Rex invited, taking pity on him.

Bertie thanked him and gulped down a generous measure. A late supper was then served to him, after which he retired to his room, wondering if his decision to flee London had been wise.

Although it was mid-December a sudden mild spell had befallen them, and it was pleasant to ride out the following morning. The trees were bare and the ground hard, but the sun had managed to shine, and there was an invigorating nip in the air. They made a merry party, Rex and Diantha, George and Elinor, with Bertie, his spirits risen to normal by the night's sound sleep in safety.

Diantha wanted to inspect some of the renovations that had been put in hand on the estate. She was delighted with what she found. The insanitary cottages had been greatly improved, and no longer threatened the health of those who lived in them. The cracks had been sealed up, so that there was real warmth from the bundles of firewood Diantha had ordered to be delivered. For the tenants, too, it would be a cheerful Christmas, the first in years. And their smiles at their new countess showed that they knew who was responsible for the change in their fortunes.

Bertie said little, but Diantha was aware of him watching everything, and herself in particular. As they turned home he moved up beside her, saying, "You did the right thing in marrying Chartridge. I doubted it before, but not now. You've come into your kingdom."

"Yes, that's how I feel," she said. "At last I have a place in the world where I belong. I might have guessed that you'd see the truth, Bertie. You have a way of seeing things."

"Well, I ain't such a fool as a lot of people think," he agreed.

"Diantha," Elinor called from her place in front. "Do you see who that is up ahead of us?"

"I believe it's Sophie," Diantha said. "And that must be Amelia with her."

Another moment and she knew she was right. The cousins from the vicarage drew closer. It was the first time Diantha had seen Sophie on horseback, as she normally used the gig to make parish calls. She was a graceful horsewoman in her plain, elegant habit, but she was cast into the shade by Amelia, splendid in dark blue velvet trimmed with silver lace.

Amelia hailed them by waving eagerly until Sophie quietly remonstrated, and soon the two parties joined up. Greetings were exchanged. Bertie's beautiful manners made him salute Sophie with as much attentiveness as he offered her beautiful cousin. But when the courtesies were over his eyes lingered on Amelia, who immediately fell in beside him, plainly considering him her property.

"Oh, dear," Sophie said softly.

"Don't fret," Diantha reassured her. "Bertie is a gentleman, and he knows she's barely out of the schoolroom."

"If only she behaved as though she were," Sophie sighed. "Unfortunately she admires Mr. Foxe greatly, and I fear this meeting has fed her admiration. What a pity he makes such a fine figure on horseback!"

"Does he?" Diantha asked in surprise. She was so used to Bertie that his looks never struck her, but watching him laughing with Amelia, she realized that he was remarkably handsome. Nor had she missed a certain softening in Sophie's voice as she spoke of him. She hoped she was mistaken. Sophie wasn't at all the sort of young woman Bertie admired, and it would be cruel for her to be hurt.

"Bertie always makes a fine figure," she said with a slight laugh. "He has an excellent tailor, who's very proud of him."

"Indeed he must be."

"I don't often see you out riding."

"Amelia wanted the ride so badly, and of course, I had to accompany her. I'm very much afraid she insisted on coming in this direction."

"Hoping to encounter Bertie. What an impression he must have made last night!"

"It wasn't just last night. She spent a few weeks in London last year, and knows of him. She says he's a great 'swell.' I fear Papa overheard her and was much shocked to hear her use such a vulgar expression. He says if Mr. Foxe is a swell, he's just the sort of young man she's been sent here to avoid. Oh, I beg your pardon. Of course, he is your cousin."

"Don't mind that," Diantha said cheerfully. "The worst I know of Bertie is that he thinks too much of his appearance. The best is that he has a good heart."

"Oh yes," Sophie said fervently. "I'm sure he has."

The party turned back toward the vicarage, and stayed awhile for tea and cakes. The Reverend Dunsford joined them, explaining that he couldn't stay long, as he was finishing his Christmas sermon. He made a small witticism in Latin, and

Bertie startled the assembled company, himself included, by capping it.

"Oh, heavens, Mr. Foxe," Amelia cried in horror. "Don't say you're bookish!"

"No, no!" he disclaimed hastily. "Had a tutor who was always quoting that. Said it every lesson. Now I can't forget it."

"I suspect Mr. Foxe is a more learned man than he wants us to know," the vicar said with a smile.

Bertie looked harassed at this slander, but didn't like to refute it more vigorously. Casting around for help, he found Sophie smiling at him, and answered her with a rueful grin.

"I look forward to seeing you all at church tomorrow," the vicar added. "Afterward, perhaps Mr. Foxe and I can dice with Horace."

"Who's Horace?" Amelia asked.

"Latin poet," Bertie said quickly. "Dreadful fellow."

On the way home he demanded to know just how early he would be required to rise from his bed. On learning that he must be downstairs by eight, he stayed pale and silent for a full ten minutes.

But next morning he presented himself perfectly attired in modest hues, and in his usual amiable temper. To Diantha's surprise he sat though the hourlong sermon with no sign of boredom.

This was more than could be said for Amelia, who sighed and looked around her. Sometimes she tried to catch Bertie's eye, and grew cross when his attention remained courteously fixed on the vicar.

When the time came to take Communion Sophie and Amelia went to the rail together. As they returned down the aisle Diantha was struck by the contrast they presented. Amelia was fidgeting with her gloves, but Sophie's face was lit by an inner glow, as though she'd been granted a glimpse of heaven.

Afterward they lingered outside the church as the congregation dispersed. Aunt Felicia made ponderous remarks about the private chapel at Ellesmere, to which none paid any heed, and the vicar engaged Bertie in conversation. Diantha tried to overhear, hoping that Bertie could give a good account of himself. He seemed to have done so, for it ended with Mr. Dunsford offering to lend him a book.

"If I can persuade my daughter to give it up," he added. "She borrowed it from me some time back, and I haven't seen it since."

"I wouldn't wish to deprive Miss Dunsford if she still has use for it," Bertie said politely.

He looked at Sophie as he spoke, but she didn't answer. The glow was still on her face, and her eyes were cast down, as though her inner vision still enchanted her. She looked up, startled. "Oh—forgive me, pray. I always become lost in the service—"

"But you have worldly duties, too, my dear," her father said gently.

It ended with them all going to the vicarage to partake of light refreshment. Bertie gave his arm to Sophie, saying that she looked faint, and Amelia promptly seized his other arm, hanging on it and flirting determinedly.

Over lunch the vicar gently quizzed Bertie, discovering that he knew an amount about the church that amazed his cousins.

"It was m'father's fault," Bertie defended himself. "He always meant me to take holy orders, being the younger son and all that."

"Now, that is something I cannot approve," Mr. Dunsford said gravely. "The church is a vocation, and it grieves me to see it used as a bolt-hole for men who need a living."

"I agree," Bertie said at once. "Tried to tell m'father that I'm not the right sort of fellow at all. But he wouldn't listen. Instructed my tutor to teach me the necessary. Luckily I had a favorite aunt. She left me a small property." He tried a weak joke. "So the church had a lucky escape."

Amelia giggled loudly. Sophie gave her gentle smile and said, "You do yourself an injustice, I'm sure, Mr. Foxe."

To Diantha's amusement Bertie reddened and quickly changed the subject. And when Amelia later twitted him on being "churchy" his smile was a little forced.

In the days that followed Bertie seemed to fit in with life at Chartridge Abbey better than Diantha had dared to hope. He was a tower of strength at the tenants' party, entertaining the children with games, tricks, and a fund of silly jokes that made his young audience roar with laughter. Diantha put much of this down to his naturally kind heart, but also to his very obvious admiration for Amelia.

"He spends too much time in her company," she said in despair to Rex.

"Does he go beyond the line?"

"No, Bertie wouldn't do that. But did he really have to teach her to drive his curricle?"

"From what I could hear, she teased him into it," Rex observed.

"But he was only too pleased. He's at the vicarage every day. I keep hoping Sophie's aunt will intervene, but she's fallen victim to Bertie's charm."

Rex grinned. "Even the vicar has started to think well of him."

"I know," Diantha said in despair. "I heard him and Sophie commending Bertie for choosing to spend Christmas quietly here, instead of indulging in rackety pleasures, like most young men." Rex gave a shout of laughter. "That's all very well," she said, aggrieved. "But I didn't know where to look. I could hardly say they were mistaken and he's only here to hide from the penalties of rackety pleasures, could I?"

"I'd have given a monkey to be there if you had," he said. "But you're right. It's best if you and I stay well out of Bertie's affairs. They're too complicated for simple souls like us."

Chapter Eight

Christmas was spent quietly, but as soon as it was over Diantha was deep in preparations for the New Year ball she was giving for the local gentry. She was relying on Sophie for advice as to the guests. Several of them had to travel some distance and must be invited for the night.

"I shall go distracted," Diantha said. "I have a whole list of people who Sophie assures me will be mortally offended if they're left out."

"You seem to be thriving on it pretty well," Rex observed. "I've never seen you in better looks."

It was true. Diantha was enjoying herself in an orgy of organizing. She'd quickly established command over her vast army of servants. "I've made the dismaying discovery that I'm a domineering female," she confided to Sophie. "Thank heavens Rex married me when he did."

"Before the dreadful truth about your character became clear, you mean?" Rex teased her. He was about to lead the gentlemen in a shooting party, and stood in the hallway with his dogs and his guns. Diantha laughed and bid him farewell.

On the night of the ball she arrayed herself in all her glory. "You will certainly be expected to do so," Rex advised her. "Anything less would be seen as a snub to the neighborhood."

So Diantha appeared in the Chartridge diamonds, recently redeemed from pawn, where the late earl had left them for so long that no one could recall their last appearance. Her dress, delivered only that morning, was of gold satin adorned with flounces of lace and with a long train. Jewels flashed from her wrists, neck, ears, and hair, and she looked truly regal.

"Magnificent," Rex declared. He raised her hand to his lips. "I chose the perfect countess."

Together they descended to where the others were waiting. Bertie looked more like his normal self, in an evening rig of positively killing elegance. Elinor wore a pale green satin underdress, with a matching net overslip. George looked a little uncomfortable in civilian evening dress, and Diantha sighed a little when she remembered how very splendid he'd been in regimentals. But Elinor's adoring eyes had no fault to find with her husband, nor he with her. In fact, when Elinor briefly flickered her frosted crepe fan in front of her face, Diantha could have sworn they stole a kiss behind it.

It was time for the ball to begin. Lord and Lady Chartridge took their place at the head of the stairs, just in front of the double doors leading to the great ballroom. There came the sound of carriages on the gravel outside, the front door was pulled open, and the footman announced the first arrivals. There was no respite for the next half hour. No one wanted to miss the first big ball given by the new earl and his wife, and every invitation had been accepted.

At last Diantha saw the vicarage party climbing the stairs. Sophie was modestly attired in a lilac crepe gown. Amelia was dressed in white, as befitted a young girl, yet her striking looks could not be concealed, and something brazen in her nature blazed forth.

"We were in two minds whether to bring her, as she isn't yet out," Sophie confided to Diantha. "But she was so determined that Aunt Felicia yielded, on the strict understanding that Amelia is not to waltz."

Amelia was already causing a sensation among the young blades, who crowded around her. Bertie was not among them. It was beneath his dignity to compete with the local swains. True, he'd stared at the vision Amelia presented, but his perfect courtesy made him claim the first dance with Sophie, and kept him at her side for several minutes, exchanging pleasantries with her and Aunt Felicia. When he formally applied to Amelia she made a great to-do about consulting her card.

"Why, sir, you come so behind the time, I fear I have few dances left." She eyed him flirtatiously. He took her card from her and scribbled on it.

In a short time everyone knew the ball was a triumphant success. The chandeliers glittered high over the dancing couples and the chaperons were seated at the sides. There were card tables in small rooms for the older men, and halfway through the evening there was a magnificent supper of jellies, creams, pies, glazed ham, lobster patties, and chicken, served with champagne.

Then it was time for the dancing to begin again. Laughing and chattering, the company trooped back into the ballroom. "May I not hope for one more dance?" Bertie asked Amelia.

She giggled. "I declare I have nothing left—except waltzes."

"Which you may not dance," Sophie reminded her gently.

"Oh, but one little waltz will do no harm. Mr. Foxe, shall we take the floor?"

But Bertie, whose behavior in all matters of ton was distinguished, shook his head regretfully. "Not for the world would I do you harm," he said. "Your guardians—"

"Oh, but I don't care for them," Amelia said, clasping her hands in her most winning style, and looking up at Bertie with an expression that would have melted a heart of stone. "Dear Mr. Foxe, you want to please me, don't you?"

"More than anything in the world," he replied gallantly. "But I fear—" He broke off in confusion. Amelia's beautiful eyes were swimming with tears.

Fortunately Rex swiftly summed up the situation and saved the day. "Miss Dawlish is promised to me," he said, drawing Amelia's arm firmly through his. "We are going to sit it out and enjoy a comfortable coze. Allow me to get you an ice, Miss Dawlish."

Amelia beamed. The earl's attention made her a person of consequence and she was able to waft away happily on his arm, pausing only to observe, "Poor Mr. Foxe. Now you have no one to waltz with. But Sophie has no partner. You can dance together until I return."

Bertie immediately solicited Sophie's hand, but she, blushing deeply, declined. "I assure you, sir, it isn't necessary. Please take no notice of what Amelia—" Embarrassment almost overcame her. "The earl is too kind," she hurried on. "I only hope he may not have jilted some other lady."

"He has," Diantha said, with a chuckle. "But since the jilted lady is myself, we need not worry."

"Then it's only right that Mr. Foxe should dance with you," Sophie said, recovering her composure.

"Stand up with my own cousin like a pair of dowdies!" Diantha exclaimed in horror. "Never!"

"By Jove, no!" Bertie agreed, with such fervor that both ladies laughed.

"Sophie, do stop being a goose and dance with Bertie," Diantha said. "You don't want everyone saying he's a wallflower, do you?"

Still blushing, Sophie allowed Bertie to lead her onto the floor. Diantha watched them as they waltzed, noticing how light and graceful Sophie was, and how remarkably pretty she looked tonight.

It was nearly four in the morning before the last carriage had rumbled away. Diantha saw to the comfort of those who were staying the night, and finally retired, with relief, to her own bedchamber. Rex joined her soon after.

"Well, what a way to use me, sir!" Dressed in a peach silk nightgown and a matching peignoir, her glorious golden hair flowing around her shoulders, Diantha surveyed her lord in mock indignation. "Jilted! Denied the dance you promised me! For shame!"

Rex laughed and kissed her bare shoulder. Diantha shivered pleasurably. "I hope your chosen companion was worth the exchange," she said.

"I had a most instructive few minutes. Miss Dawlish is a minx and a rather vulgar young woman, both empty-headed and ill bred. But she possesses ten thousand pounds of her own. She tells this to anyone who will listen. So I fear we may yet find ourselves connected with her."

"Bertie?"

"I believe he needs an heiress badly. Ten thousand isn't a vast fortune, but I don't think he can afford to be choosy."

"Besides, he's vastly taken with her looks," Diantha sighed. "Oh, dear!"

"Now, I refuse to spend another moment discussing a young woman who interests me so little," Rex declared. "Having neglected you earlier, it is clearly my duty to pay you much attention now." He drew her to her feet and tossed the elegant peignoir to the floor, drawing her into his arms. Diantha raised her face for his kiss, and like him, consigned all other thoughts to perdition.

January was hard and cold, with bitter winds that drove people indoors. Amelia spent much time languishing on a sofa, lamenting the want of amusements in the locality. She disliked accompanying Sophie on her parish visits, and couldn't persuade her to abandon them to keep her entertained.

"She doesn't seem to find Bertie's attentions entertainment enough," Diantha mused. "That doesn't augur well for their marriage. Let's hope he sees the danger in time."

"I hope I'm not uncharitable," Elinor responded, "but the thought of taking Amelia into the family is not pleasant."

They were out riding together, leaving the groom behind and enjoying each other's company as in the days of their unmarried girlhood. A visit to the village assured Diantha that all was well, and then, as the sky was darkening, they turned back to the Abbey. With barely half a mile to go they observed a carriage coming their way, which proved to contain Amelia and Aunt Felicia. It slowed to a halt near them, and Amelia leaned out.

"I'll be going home in a couple of days," she called. "So I'm making my good-byes in proper form now."

"That's very kind," Diantha said, "but you're dining with us tomorrow night."

"Oh yes, I forgot." Amelia shrugged. Her sharp eyes flickered between them. "Isn't Mr. Foxe with you?"

Diantha looked surprised. "I'd assumed he was with you. I'm sure he said he was going to the vicarage today."

"Why, look!" Elinor said.

They all turned and saw Bertie's curricle appearing in the distance. He was driving his three horses random tandem, and making a very pretty job of it, but what drew Diantha's attention was the sight of Sophie sitting beside him.

Amelia, too, seemed quite taken aback. "I declare," she said coolly, "I had no idea Mr. Foxe was taking my cousin driving. How vastly good-natured of him."

Diantha's eyes snapped at this rudeness. "Miss Dunsford's elegance of mind is such that she must command admiration wherever she goes," she said firmly.

"Oh, to be sure," Amelia said in a bored tone. "But such a dowd. Besides, she disapproves of him. Lord knows what they found to talk of!"

Diantha, too, would have given much to know the answer to that question. Neither Sophie nor Bertie looked in the least bored with each other. He was talking with a smile on his face, and Sophie was listening intently, her cheeks becomingly flushed.

When they had drawn up Sophie said, "Mr. Foxe was so kind as to take me parish visiting. I'm afraid it has been a dull afternoon for him."

"No such thing," Bertie declared at once. "I don't know when I've enjoyed myself more."

Amelia giggled. "What would they say of you in London if they heard that?"

Bertie looked surprised. "It's strange, but I haven't given London a thought," he confessed. He clutched his hat as he spoke, for a sharp wind had sprung up.

"Surely you're longing to get back to your exciting life." Amelia pouted. "It's so dull down here. How can you bear it?"

"Well, well," he said, humoring her, "London's all very fine in its way."

"I shall be going to London, soon," Amelia said pointedly. "I declare, I can't wait."

Bertie gave her a small bow. "I hope you find it everything you expect. *Hey!*" His dignified speech ended in a yelp as the wind buffeted him again, sweeping his beaver off its nicely calculated angle on his polished locks. He made a wild grab for it, but it went bowling away down a small slope.

"Hang it!" he cried.

"I'll take the reins," Sophie said, taking them from him.

He gave her a smile of gratitude and sprang down from the curricle. They watched him sprint after the hat, which always managed to keep just in front of him. Diantha chuckled at the sight of his frantic figure so nearly catching the hat, and always defeated at the last minute, and even the kindly Sophie had to smile.

Amelia jumped down from the carriage and sauntered over to her. Her mouth was pursed in a way that spoiled its beauty, and hinted at the shrew she would one day become. "I declare, I'm vastly surprised," she said affectedly. "Mr. Foxe is so particular who he allows to drive his cattle."

"Oh, I wouldn't try to drive them," Sophie said. "Just to hold them for him. I'm not skilled with the ribbons, like you, Amelia."

"Yes, he says I'm going to be a very pretty whip,"

Amelia said complacently. "He even lets me drive them random tandem."

Diantha's eyes opened wide, for she'd heard Bertie tell how Amelia had pleaded to be taught to drive three horses, and he'd refused. She kept silent, however, feeling that she could hardly call Amelia a liar to her face.

But the next moment she wished she'd done so, for Amelia sprang up into the curricle, seized the reins from Sophie, and cried, "Here, let me show you!" Before anyone could stop her, she'd started the horses.

It was immediately clear that her boasts were idle. The high-strung animals, sensing her uncertain touch, shied and skittered, and hurried away, ignoring her frantic efforts to bring them under control. Aunt Felicia screamed.

"Oh, Diantha," Elinor gasped, "what shall we do?"

"Ride," Diantha said grimly.

In a moment they were after the curricle. They could hear Amelia's terrified shrieks floating back to them, and see Sophie clinging on for dear life as the vehicle bounced and bumped, going faster and faster, the horses reveling in their sudden freedom.

On the slope below, Bertie looked up in horror to see the curricle swaying violently toward him. He shouted something, but the wind whipped it away. Then he was running forward in a desperate attempt to intercept the animals. But he never reached them. The wheels struck a rock and the unwieldy vehicle lurched to one side. The horses lost their footing, and the next moment the curricle had turned over into a ditch.

Diantha would always remember the horror of the next few seconds. Nothing moved in the ditch as she and Elinor rode up, but then, mercifully, they saw Amelia stir and begin to crawl out. They reached out their arms to help her up the bank. Her dress was torn and she was sobbing wildly. She turned as Bertie arrived, expecting to be comforted. But he passed her by without a second look, to throw himself down into the ditch with an agonized cry of "Sophie! Oh my God—*Sophie*!"

She had been thrown clear and lay still. Oblivious to the damage to his clothes, Bertie climbed over the smashed curricle and dropped beside her. "Sophie," he cried again, touching her gently.

To everyone's vast relief, Sophie moved a little and opened her eyes. "I'm not hurt," she whispered, "not really."

With a sob Bertie gathered her into his arms, holding her close and rocking back and forth. Diantha and Elinor stared at him, and then at each other, in astonishment.

"Help me," he cried, distraught.

"We're not too far from the Abbey," Diantha said. "We'll take her there in the carriage and send someone for a doctor."

"I'm all right," Sophie said feebly. "I can walk."

"No," Bertie said firmly. "You're not going to walk."

He helped Sophie carefully to her feet. Mercifully there seemed to be no bones broken, but as soon as she was upright she swayed dizzily against Bertie. He clasped her firmly, raised her in his arms, and climbed out of the ditch, carrying her.

By this time the Dunsfords' coachman had turned his unwieldy vehicle and lumbered toward them. Amelia's cries had risen to shrieks, less of pain than of temper at being ignored. She cast herself into Aunt Felicia's arms, bawling loudly. Elinor went to try to soothe her, but to no avail.

They managed to get Sophie settled into the

coach, but she clung to Bertie, murmuring, "Don't leave me."

"Never," he declared passionately. "Never in life!"

Then, having astonished everyone, he astonished them still further by placing a gentle but determined kiss on Sophie's mouth. The vicar's daughter didn't seem shocked by this forward behavior; instead she returned the kiss, and rested her head against his shoulder.

Diantha spurred her horse and raced ahead of them to the Abbey. In minutes a servant was galloping off for the doctor, another one went for the vicar, and the housekeeper was having a chamber prepared for Sophie.

After what seemed like an endless wait the carriage arrived. Bertie climbed out and immediately lifted Sophie in his arms. As luck would have it the Reverend Dunsford came galloping up at that moment, arriving just in time to see Bertie carry his daughter inside and up the stairs. He saw, too, the way Sophie nestled against Bertie, her arms wrapped confidingly about his neck, and a shadow crossed his face.

"You can leave her with us now," Diantha said when Bertie had lowered Sophie onto the bed. "See, her father is here."

Explanations had to wait until the doctor had been and attended to both Sophie and Amelia. Neither was seriously hurt, but it was settled that Sophie would remain at the Abbey overnight. Amelia was declared well enough to return home, which she seemed to take as an insult.

"I don't see why everyone's making such a fuss about Sophie," she snuffled. "I declare I had a much worse time than she."

Then, to everyone's astonishment, Bertie, that pink of the ton, famed for the elegance of his manners, rose and faced her, his eyes cold. "That ain't true," he said bluntly. "And if it were true, you selfish little brat, it would be no more than you deserve. How *dare* you put Miss Dunsford at risk! By God, it's well for you that she's not seriously hurt!"

Amelia gaped, then burst into a loud wail. "But you like *me*," she sobbed.

"Like you?" he echoed scathingly. "Do you think I'd look at you when *she* was near? Do you think I came to call on you? I came because I couldn't stay away from her—"

The vicar rose hastily. "I think this had better wait until another time," he said in a strained voice. "Lady Chartridge, I know I can leave my daughter in your hands with an easy mind."

He departed with Amelia and Aunt Felicia, leaving a stunned silence behind him.

"Well!" Diantha exclaimed. "I was never more astonished in my life."

The vicar called for Sophie the following day. They traveled in the carriage, with Bertie riding behind. He was gone some hours, and returned in despair.

"I begged him for Sophie's hand," he said. "But . . ." He shrugged.

"He said no?" Diantha echoed. "But Mr. Dunsford likes you."

Bertie gave a short laugh. "Well enough. But he's no fool. He says I'm a dandy with extravagant ways, volatile, and quite unsuitable to marry a girl like Sophie."

"The same thought had occurred to me," she murmured. "You do have debts, and I believe Sophie's fortune isn't large."

"I thought of selling that little property of mine. It should cover the debts. As for supporting her—

well . . ." Bertie gave an awkward laugh. "Perhaps my father's idea wasn't so wild after all."

"You? In holy orders?"

"I'm in love with Sophie," Bertie said simply. "I'll do anything to be worthy of her."

"How does she feel?"

A glow came into Bertie's face. "She loves me, too. She pleaded with her father to sanction our betrothal."

"But he remained adamant?" Diantha asked sympathetically.

"Not totally," Bertie admitted. "He says he needs time to consider. We can see each other, but not alone, and there must be no talk of marriage."

"Well then, just be patient, and he'll come around," Diantha rallied him. "Rex and I will do all we can to help. Don't give up hope."

It seemed that Bertie's ordeal wasn't to be so very terrible. Over the next couple of weeks the two families continued to dine together, and at an informal ball given at Chartridge Abbey, Sophie was permitted to stand up with Bertie for a country dance, though not to waltz with him. It was clear that the vicar was watching them together, and Diantha felt that he must be impressed by the picture they presented. Their love blazed from them, their eyes met constantly. Sophie, who valued a man's inner worth, had somehow found what she was seeking in this apparently feckless young man. And Bertie, the swell, the young blood who'd always been game for any lark, was at the feet of a demure, Quakerish young woman, whose only allure was a pair of beautiful, honest eyes.

Sometimes Diantha regarded him in comic dismay. She'd thought that Bertie at least would stay free of the irrational snares of love. She began to wonder if she herself was the only strong-minded person in the world.

She'd ventured to mention the matter to Mr. Dunsford, and found him troubled but not unsympathetic.

"If Bertie takes orders, wouldn't that meet the case?" she asked.

He shook his head. "Will it seem strange to you, Lady Chartridge, that it is that suggestion that disturbs me more than any other? You know my feelings on the taking of orders for convenience. I would need to know of some other reason, a true vocation, before I could consent."

But then his eyes softened as he looked at Bertie and Sophie playing spillikins together, laughing together over their silly mistakes. "But I believe he loves my child truly, and I cannot be indifferent to that." He gave a little sigh. "My own marriage was exceedingly happy."

And that evening before he left, he lingered, talking to Rex so that the lovers might have a few minutes alone.

"I think the vicar is beginning to see what an excellent person Bertie truly is," Elinor said later that night, when they were all lingering before going to bed. "He spoke to you very kindly tonight, Bertie."

"He did, didn't he?" Bertie said eagerly. "I think I may begin to hope." He sighed. "It'll be all up with me if I don't win her."

"I can remember when you spoke of your neckcloths like that," Diantha teased.

He grinned. "That was when I thought neckcloths important."

The gilt clock on the mantelpiece had just struck eleven when they heard carriage wheels on the gravel outside, and the sound of doors being slammed.

"Who can be calling at this hour?" Diantha asked.

The next moment a footman entered and spoke to Diantha. "There are two—er—persons in the hall, desiring to speak with your ladyship."

"Persons?" she queried, noting that the footman didn't say "lady" or "gentleman." Clearly these were people who wouldn't normally expect to be received at Chartridge Abbey. "What are their names?"

"Mr. and Mrs. Templeton, your ladyship."

Standing just in front of Bertie, Diantha clearly heard him gulp. Her eyes met Rex's in a shared moment of amusement. George pressed his lips together, and even the gentle Elinor covered her mouth with her hand, for Diantha had shared the secret with her.

"Please show them in," Diantha said.

Bertie shifted uneasily. "Er—perhaps—"

"Stay where you are," she said firmly.

The little company stood in suspended animation while the footman left the room and returned with a very large man, dressed in clothes that had once been costly in a rather showy style. Beside him trotted a young woman who, at the sight of Bertie, gave a little cry and flew across the room, arms outstretched. He backed up a step, but sheer good breeding prevented him from totally repulsing her, and the next moment she'd cast herself onto his breast, moaning, "Bertie, my love. How could you abandon me?"

Bertie tried to speak, but it was hard when he was being choked by a pair of frantically clutching arms. At last a few strangulated words made their escape. "Beg you, ma'am—mistake—never dream of—no, really—'pon my soul—"

"Wretch!" shouted the big man. "Seducer! Despoiler of innocent women!"

"No I ain't!" Bertie squealed. "Dashed well never spoiled an innocent woman in my life. And she wasn't. Innocent, I mean. If she *had* been, I wouldn't have—hang it all, Sidonia, let go of me, there's a good girl."

With an effort he freed himself. Sidonia promptly gave a shriek and fell to the floor, kneeling there, looking upward in theatrical appeal. She was small and dainty, and Diantha's first thought was that there had been a mistake. Surely this fragile doll, whose blond curls peeped out from beneath the brim of her velvet bonnet, couldn't be the hardened temptress of Bertie's tale? But a closer glance revealed that Sidonia Templeton's face was a good deal older than it seemed at first glance, and had the unhealthy color of one who lived much by candlelight. Or perhaps it was just that she didn't wash very often. The grubbiness of her lace collar made this likely.

She became aware of Diantha's shrewd gaze and looked up, revealing her pale eyes in all their cold, hard reality. Then she quickly buried her face in her handkerchief again, wailing, "How can you so forget your promises?"

"Never forgot my promises—never made any," Bertie declared with perfect truth. "It was you who—I mean, when we—oh, Lord!" His voice trailed away in despair.

Mr. Templeton turned to the assembled company, his hands thrown out in appeal. "Ladies, gentleman, you see before you a brokenhearted husband. While I was unavoidably called from town, leaving my darling innocent little wife behind—ah, that I should have been so incautious! But how could I have known that her virtue would be assailed by a wolf in sheep's clothing?"

"Here, who are you calling a sheep?" Bertie yelped.

"No, Bertie dear," Diantha murmured. "He's calling you a wolf. It's a step up—I think."

Her cousin turned to her with an agonized expression. Rex, admirably preserving a straight face, murmured in his wife's ear, "This is a thoroughly improper scene for ladies. I think you and Elinor should retire."

An indignant glance from Diantha's flashing eyes met him. "Dismiss that from your mind, my lord," she murmured back. "Nothing would prevail upon me to miss such promising entertainment."

"You are shameless, madam," he declared in a censorious voice that made her chuckle.

Instantly Mr. Templeton turned on her. "Ah, you think it a subject for jest, but I appeal to you, as a woman, take pity on my darling. Exert yourself to preserve her good name."

"What exactly did you come here in the hope of obtaining?" Rex demanded dryly.

"Satisfaction," Mr. Templeton declared dramatically.

"I fail to see how a duel will preserve your darling's good name," Rex observed. "More likely to muddy it."

"True. I abhor violence. The satisfaction I had in mind was of a different kind."

"Ah! I see."

There was a warning note in Rex's voice if Mr. Templeton had possessed the wit to hear it. But he'd reached the dramatic moment of a speech probably used many times before in similar circumstances, and he was intent on getting to the end.

"I have forgiven my treasure her infidelity," he

cried. "For I know that she is not the one to blame. She has been abused, deceived by a heartless seducer—"

"No such thing," declared Bertie, whose spirit had revived when he learned that no violence was contemplated. "If there's been any deceiving done—I spent a fortune on this rapacious little lovebird. Did you see those sapphires she nagged me into giving her? She knew I was already deep in debt, but nothing would please her but to have them. Now I'm in deeper still. And all the time she had a partner in crime ready to blackmail me."

"Oh!" Sidonia screamed. "How can you speak so, after what we've been to each other?"

But Bertie made no response. He seemed to have been turned to stone. One by one the others turned to follow his petrified gaze to the door, where stood the Reverend Dunsford and Sophie, her face pale and distraught.

Chapter Nine

It was Rex who first regained his presence of mind. "You're mistaken, Bertie," he grated. "It isn't you who is being blackmailed, but us. Or rather, my wife. I'll wager this prize pair laid their plans on the day after our marriage." He seized Sidonia by the elbows and hauled her up. "It's nothing but a scheme to get their hands on a slice of the Halstow fortune. You were merely the victim. But you've missed your mark, my beauties. Not a penny. Now or ever. George, be so good as to summon a magistrate."

"Very willingly," George replied.

Templeton's smile was ghastly. "Come, come—no need to be hasty. A misunderstanding. We make no accusations, lay no charges—in fact, now I come to see Mr. Foxe in a better light, I feel sure it was someone else entirely. If I might have a little brandy—"

"What you may have," said Rex deliberately, "is five minutes' head start. Now, get out."

Sidonia scuttled out, brushing past Sophie, who drew her skirts instinctively aside. Her face was dreadfully pale. Watching her, Diantha knew that she'd heard too much for Rex's covering fire to have achieved its purpose.

Templeton fled in his wife's wake, followed by Rex and George, and from the hallway came the sounds of ejection. Diantha took Sophie's hands in hers and did her best for Bertie. "I'm sorry you had to see that unsavory pair. Poor Bertie . . ." Her voice faded. It was useless.

"I think we, too, should take our departure," the Reverend Dunsford said firmly.

"No, you must stay," Diantha said in alarm.

"No, thank you," said Sophie. "Forgive me if I seem rude, but—I must go."

"But surely—"

"I heard," Sophie interrupted her fiercely. "Don't you understand? I heard everything." Her beautiful eyes, full of torment, turned on Bertie.

He seemed to be fighting for breath. "Miss Dunsford—" he pleaded. "Sophie—if you'd only let me explain—"

"There can be no reason for you to offer me explanations, Mr. Foxe," Sophie returned with quiet dignity. "Your life is no concern of mine, and I would never be so impertinent as to believe that it could be."

"But I want it to be," he cried. "I want to marry you, Sophie."

"I must decline your flattering offer, Mr. Foxe. We have nothing in common. I could not—" a wintry smile passed briefly over Sophie's face "—enter into your friendships."

"But that's all over," he said frantically. "It was over before I knew you. Sophie, it's not so very bad. I've lived the way men in my set live, but a fellow gives all that up when he marries a decent girl."

The Reverend Dunsford spoke. "And why, sir, should a 'fellow' expect a decent girl to marry such a man as yourself? A man who spends money that is not his to buy the favors of a light woman. We returned to inform you that my daughter had prevailed upon me to agree to your marriage, but after what I have seen here tonight, let me tell you that nothing would make me consent."

"Father, take me home," Sophie begged in a suffocating voice.

"Come, my dear. We do not belong here." The vicar put his arm around his daughter and drew her gently away.

In the days following, a shadow lay over Chartridge Abbey. No one doubted that Sophie's refusal was irrevocable. Gentle she might be, but she had her father's firm character. It could outface anything, even her own love.

Bertie walked around looking like a dead man. His chance had come and gone so quickly that it had left him stunned. Once Diantha, walking in the grounds, came across him sitting on a log, staring into the distance. He didn't hear her approach at first, then he looked up briefly before returning to his thoughts.

"Bertie dear, don't sit out here in the cold," she begged. "This is so unlike you."

"I *am* unlike me," he said morosely. "I'm so different from my old self that it's like being another man entirely. Sophie did that to me. With her I became—oh, better than I am. And I could have stayed better, with her help. And then, to have something rise up from a past that no longer seems a part of me—" He dropped his head into his hands.

Diantha regarded him in helpless sympathy. When he didn't raise his head she touched him gently on the shoulder and returned home without him.

In the morning room she met George reading a sporting paper. When she told him about Bertie he nodded kindly. "Bad business," he said. "That kind of woman can do so much damage."

Diantha smiled. "George dear, you're beginning to sound middle-aged."

"So I am," he said, startled. "It's the effects of a happy marriage."

"I regard my own marriage as happy," she said indignantly. "And Rex is *not* getting middle-aged."

He grinned. "No, not Rex. Best thing he ever did was to marry you. At least *he* never—that is—well, anyway—"

Diantha's eyebrows lifted. "You're not telling me that Rex has a Sidonia Templeton in his past? I feel sure he dealt with her quite ruthlessly."

"It was a long time ago," George said, looking harassed.

"Then there's no harm in your telling me." George set his chin in silence. "Or I could ask Rex," Diantha mused.

"Look here," George said, alarmed, "you mustn't tell him that I even mentioned—"

"Well, if you tell me about it, there'll be no need for me to say anything to him," she pointed out reasonably. "Was she like that creature?"

"In some ways. I only met her once. Her name was Lady Bartlett, and she was supposed to be unassailable. Rex simply fell for her, head over heels. I've never seen him so deeply . . . well . . ." George seemed to become aware whom he was addressing, and colored.

"It's all right," Diantha told him. "As you say, it was a long time ago." Something was happening to her heart. Its thumping had become suddenly erratic, and she knew that whatever might happen, she *had* to hear the end of this story. "Did Lord Bartlett try to blackmail Rex?" she asked lightly.

"No, nothing like that. Rex always knew she was

married. He simply worshiped her from afar, and didn't try to—that is—"

"Didn't try to make her his mistress?" Diantha supplied.

"That's right. In fact, he was so discreet that nobody except me ever knew how he felt about her."

"What a charming tale," Diantha said in a brittle voice. "How did it end?"

"He used to write her poetry. One night he went to her house. Her husband was away and Rex thought she was at the theater. He meant to leave his poems on her pillow. He slipped into the house without anyone seeing, crept up to her room, and went inside."

"Well?" Diantha asked in agony, for George had paused uncomfortably.

"She was there. Only she wasn't alone. There was a man with her."

"Not her husband, I take it?"

"Not her husband."

Diantha forced a smile to lips that suddenly felt stiff. "Do you mean that Rex actually discovered them in *flagrante delicto*?"

"Eh? No, they were in bed," George said blankly.

She drew a deep breath. "It means the same."

"Oh yes. They were that, all right. After the way he treated her," George brooded, "putting her on a pedestal, idealizing her, worshiping her as some chaste idol, and all the time she—"

"She wasn't chaste at all. What did he do?"

"Backed out of the room and closed the door as quietly as he could. It was dark and they never even knew he'd been and gone. Afterward we heard that Lord Bartlett had arrived home later the same night and found the man still there. He challenged him to a duel, and shot him dead. The Bartletts fled the country. Rex never saw her again. You can imagine what it did to him."

"Yes," she said slowly.

George colored awkwardly. "Diantha, I shouldn't have told you any of this. If Rex knew, he'd be fit to boil me in oil. You won't—?"

"No. I won't tell him you told me, ever."

To her relief Rex was out, and she was free to run upstairs to her own room. She locked the door behind her and leaned on it, trying to come to terms with the storm of feeling that had swept over her.

Now she understood so many things, including the savage look in Rex's eyes the night they'd met, when he hinted at a contempt for women. The cool face he presented to the world was but a mask. Rex's true self had grown from the heartsick boy whose adored idol had mocked and deceived him. And now she realized how completely he'd hidden this self from her.

She found that she was shaking, and clasped her hands together to control them. What did all this matter to her? She'd made a marriage of convenience with a man who no more loved her than she loved him. That was their bargain, and they'd both kept it. She had no complaint.

"I don't care," she muttered. "Why should I care? It's all so long ago. I must have been a child. He can have been little more than a boy. It has nothing to do with Rex and me, now."

But the bitter jealousy in her heart gnawed at her. Once Rex had softened with tenderness for a woman. Once there had been love in his heart.

Pain slashed at Diantha with savage claws. She tried to fight it off with her old weapons, reason and good sense. But reason was useless against the tide of emotion that engulfed her. It made no difference that it had all been long ago. Rex had worshiped this woman, and it had destroyed him. What was left was a shell that walked and talked but could never love again.

He'd offered her a dead heart because that was all she'd asked for, and in her stupidity and ignorance she hadn't known that it mattered. But Rex had known. The night he found her with her father's letters he'd castigated himself in words whose significance had escaped her.

He let her believe she could live without love, when he knew different. . . . If he'd had a shred of decency, he'd have turned away from her, but . . . he let her walk into disaster with a smile on her face.

He'd called their marriage a disaster for her, because he was indifferent to her, and he'd feared the day when she might come to want more.

"But I don't," she told herself desperately. "I don't love him. My marriage is happy as it is, very happy."

The walls threw back her words in mocking echo. The mirror showed her to herself, a woman distraught at the discovery of her own love for a man whose heart could never be hers.

"No," she cried aloud. "It isn't true! I'm not in love with him! I'm not! *I'm not!*"

In some far distant universe she thought she heard mocking laughter.

It was evening before she saw Rex again. They were giving a small dinner for the squire, the local mayor, and their wives. Rex entered her room wearing evening dress that was neat and elegant without being showy. Her heart gave a painful thump at this first sight of him since she'd understood the truth about her own feelings. How handsome he was! How broad of shoulder and long of leg! She'd noticed those details the very first day in Hyde Park, but failed to understand her own response. Now, with her sensuality awakened, she knew that she'd wanted him from the start.

He gave her his usual smile, and she had to fight not to let her reaction show on her face. His eyes were warm and friendly, but without ardor.

"Ready, my lady?" he asked lightly.

"Quite ready." She took his hand, hoping that he wouldn't feel her trembling.

But perhaps he did feel it, because he lifted her chin and looked down into her eyes, with concern. "You're looking pale. Are you ill?"

"Just a little tired after Christmas," she said with a forced laugh. "And being so sad about Bertie . . ."

"Yes, a bad business. George and I thought we'd take him to visit some friends who have a hunting lodge near here. It might help to shake him out of himself. You can spend the time restfully with Elinor. You wouldn't mind if we were away a week?"

"You're free as air, my lord."

He smiled. "You always make the right answer. I married the perfect wife."

The perfect wife, she thought as they went downstairs. *One who makes no demands on you, who will never ask you to love her.*

She put her head up. She'd made her bargain and she was too proud to complain.

That night she lay awake, aching for Rex to come to her. But when he did so, she froze. She was suddenly terrified to make love with him, lest she give herself away. At all costs she must avoid embarrassing him with feelings that he didn't want. She tried to force herself to appear normal, but Rex couldn't mistake her awkwardness. He gave his usual ironic smile.

"I don't mean to force myself on you, m'dear. You must be wishing me at the devil. Get some rest now."

He kissed her kindly and left with no sign of resentment for her unresponsiveness. Diantha waited until he was gone. Then she thumped the pillow as hard as she could in despair and frustration at having become that most ridiculous of creatures: a woman in love with her own husband.

At the end of January George and Elinor departed for Ainsley Court, and Bertie returned to London. Rex and Diantha remained at Chartridge Abbey for another two months, overseeing work on the estate. Occasionally George and Elinor returned for a few days and the four would spend a happy weekend together.

After the first shock of discovering that she was in love with Rex, Diantha's courage had revived, and she decided that her situation didn't look so black after all. She was married to him, constantly in his company. They had their private jokes, which were very sweet to her. And at night they had their passion.

When he returned from hunting she went back into his arms, sure now that she wouldn't give herself away. No man's heart was dead forever, she reasoned. She had time to win him. So her spirits rose, and the next few weeks passed happily enough.

Then Delaney, coming from London with papers for Rex's signature, brought news that wiped everything else from their minds.

"Bonaparte has escaped from Elba," he declared, holding out a copy of the *Times*.

Rex glanced briefly at the newspaper, which was two days old, and merely carried the news of the escape. "Nothing more recent than this?" he asked. "What do the bankers say?"

Delaney nodded. "Rothschilds, of course, have their own intelligence network. It reports that Bonaparte has reached France and is being welcomed with open arms. The whole continent is in uproar. It means war, Rex. We thought it was all over, but now I fear the worst battle is yet to come."

George and Elinor happened to be staying at the Abbey. George took the paper from his brother's hand and turned away with it. Elinor was watching him, her face pale.

"If it's war," George said slowly, "Wellington will need every man. But half the army has been sent to America."

He raised his head to look directly at his wife. Elinor saw his purpose in his eyes, and her hands flew to her face. Without a word George walked away, and after a moment she went after him.

"What does he mean to do?" Diantha asked.

"I rather think he means to rejoin the army," Rex said.

"The regiment has already been ordered to Brussels," Delaney said. "They leave in a week."

"I think the time has come for us all to go back to London," Rex said.

George and Elinor returned to Ainsley Court and from there traveled to London independently. Diantha guessed they wanted to make the journey alone together, not knowing how much more time they might have. Rex told them to put up at Chartridge House until George was sent abroad, after which he expected Elinor to remain with Diantha and himself. He had estate business to attend first, and made the journey with Diantha two days later.

They reached home in the middle of the afternoon. As soon as Elinor heard their arrival she came flying down to throw her arms around Diantha's neck. The cousins held each other in silence for a long moment, then Diantha said, "Come upstairs, love, and tell me everything."

In her bedroom Elinor burst into tears. "George has rejoined," she wept. "I try to be brave. I never let him see me cry. But oh, Diantha, how can I bear it? We've had such a little time together."

"And you'll have many years more." Diantha tried to rally her. "Why, you goose, they'll capture Boney and send him back."

Elinor shook her head. "You haven't yet heard the latest rumors in London. They say Paris received him with cheers, and there's going to be a great battle. George leaves soon and I want to go with him, but he won't let me. That *proves* it's dangerous."

"All it proves is that you shouldn't be left to live almost alone in a strange city," Diantha said cheerfully.

"As though I cared about that! Oh, Diantha, once he's gone to battle I may never see him again. I must be with him while I can. It doesn't matter where I live. Anywhere will do—a tent."

Diantha smiled at these wild fantasies. "Are you going to follow the drum?" she asked lightly.

"Yes, if I have to," Elinor said at once. "I *must* be with George."

Diantha's humor died as she recognized in Elinor's face a reckless resolution that had never been there before. Her gentle cousin, always before so easily swayed, meant every word she uttered.

"Wait," Diantha said. "I have a plan. We'll talk

later." She left Elinor's room and hurried away to think.

Rex's face, when he returned, told its own story. "War," he said simply. "And this time the whole of Europe will go up in flames. Already the regiments are gathering in Brussels."

"Then so should we," Diantha said at once. "Elinor wants to be near George, and I think we should be there with him, too."

Rex frowned. "I'd planned to go myself, but as for allowing women—"

"Good heavens, the battle isn't going to be tomorrow, is it?"

"Of course not. It will take weeks, months, to get everything into place."

"And in the meantime anything of any interest is going to happen in Brussels," she said gaily. "Where else should we be?" She snapped her fingers. "That for Boney!"

His brow cleared. "What a woman I married! Perhaps Boney should be warned about you. It might send him scuttling back to Elba."

It was a merry gathering at dinner that night. Elinor was full of joy at being able to follow George, and her eyes constantly caressed her husband.

"I wonder where Bertie is," Rex mused after a while. "I sent a message to his rooms inviting him to dine with us tonight."

"It's certainly unlike Bertie to lose the chance to dine at someone else's expense," Diantha agreed. "Perhaps he's encountered the Templetons."

"I feel sorry for the Templetons if he did," Rex observed.

It wasn't until they were all taking tea, an hour later, that Bertie appeared. "You wretch," Diantha chided him. Then the smile died from her face. "Why, Bertie, whatever's happened?" His face was pale and calm, and something about it frightened her. She went to him, taking both his hands in hers. "Tell me," she insisted.

"I came to say good-bye," he said quietly. "I've joined up as a volunteer in George's regiment."

"You?" She tried to restrain the unflattering astonishment in her voice, but it came out. He gave her a wan smile.

"Yes, me. Bertie Foxe, who never paid for his clothes or his dinner in his life, if he could help it: who thought of nothing but his own pleasure. But you see, I don't care for that anymore." He added simply, "I don't care for anything now I've lost Sophie."

"Oh, Bertie." Diantha put her arms about her cousin. Rex rose and shook his hand, followed by George. They drew him closer to the fire, and George soothed the ladies by explaining that Bertie hadn't enlisted as a private soldier, with all its accompanying hardships.

"A volunteer is a gentleman," George said. "And he lives as a gentleman, taking his meals with the officers. I'll keep an eye on him. Don't worry."

But Bertie's action disturbed Diantha as nothing else so far had done. The memory of his face as he said, *"I don't care for anything now I've lost Sophie,"* stayed with her and troubled her. Bertie, whose light-o'-loves had been legion, had succumbed to a feeling so strong that his life was nothing to him in comparison. Then Elinor's face, too, came into her mind. How her eyes had glowed with possessive passion as they rested on George; she was ready to follow him to the ends of the earth, laughing at danger or discomfort as long as he was there.

These days Diantha understood the force that moved them. It was as though a curtain had drawn back, revealing a world that had always been there, but that she'd been too blind to see. She wished she could have talked about her feelings to Rex, as they'd talked about everything in the old days. But the knowledge that she loved him, while he didn't love her, threw a shadow between them. Mostly she kept her spirits up, telling herself that one day he would be hers. But sometimes a shiver went through her, and she dreaded that that day might never come.

At the heart of the Belgian capital lay the Parc de Bruxelles. It was a huge, elegant garden, criss-crossed with paths, giving splendid perspectives to two ornamental pools crowned by fountains. On one side stood the royal palace. At right angles to it ran the Rue Royale, in which stood the allied headquarters, hastily being made ready for the arrival of the Duke of Wellington. On the far side of the park was the Rue Ducale, lined with spacious mansions, and it was one of these that Delaney, sent on ahead, leased for Lord Chartridge and his family.

Diantha was delighted with the house with its views over the park, where society promenaded every day. A suite was assigned to Elinor and George, and a couple of rooms to Bertie and his valet. He thanked her quietly. He seemed lost these days, and clung to his military duties as the focus of an otherwise aimless life.

Diantha soon realized that Rex had been right when he said that nothing would happen for weeks. A sense of urgency had driven them across the channel, but once they were in Brussels, the urgency fell away. A great army was gathering to decide the fate of Europe, but while it did so, life consisted of balls, breakfasts, rides in the countryside, and whatever other amusements occurred to people starved of foreign travel. Much of English high society was already there. More was arriving by the day.

Diantha was an immediate success. Her beauty and dashing ways made her a favorite with the men, and she quickly embarked on several desperate flirtations. But if she'd hoped to make her husband jealous, she was disappointed. Rex regarded her antics with cynical amusement. Occasionally he would blight the pretensions of a lovesick swain with a raised eyebrow and a look whose meaning was unmistakable. Apart from that he didn't interfere.

With a whole new society to conquer, it was naturally necessary to order a new wardrobe. Diantha made a call on Madame Fillon, who made clothes for the ladies of the Belgian royal family, and placed a massive order for tea gowns, ballgowns, and promenade dresses. Naturally this entailed buying shoes, stockings, shawls, fans, and hats, and somehow the first few weeks slipped away in a riot of fittings and visits to silk warehouses.

As March turned into April the weather grew suddenly a good deal warmer, and almost every day there was a picnic or a military review to watch. Apart from the British, the allied army consisted of Dutch, Belgians, Hanoverians, and Prussians. The city was filling up with foreign uniforms, and each country vied with the others to put on the most impressive parade. George's and Bertie's duties seemed to consist almost entirely of these ceremonial occasions, and their female relations made a point of going to admire them.

At the start of April, to everyone's relief, the Duke of Wellington arrived and the preparations for battle moved into a higher gear. But few suspected the seething activity that went on at headquarters late into the night. Life in society went on exactly the same, except that it, too, became more feverish and urgent. The duke enjoyed parties, both giving and attending them. He was also reputed to be a fervent admirer of the ladies, and no beauty, however notorious, could complain of the great man's neglect.

Stories began to be told of him. It was said that while compiling a list of guests for one of his own soirees, the duke had been discreetly warned that a certain lady should not be included, since her character was "suspicious."

"Is it, by Jove!" he exclaimed. "Then I'll go and ask her myself." And he did so, within the hour.

"The Duke of Wellington," wrote one outraged matron, "has not improved the *morality* of our society." Which was true, and did nothing to stem the frantic gaiety that illuminated Brussels throughout those weeks.

The slightly dissipated atmosphere was intensified by the news that Lord Uxbridge was to join Wellington to command the cavalry. Uxbridge was a fine soldier, but he'd had an adulterous liaison with the wife of Wellington's brother, which culminated in them running away together. But when reminded of this the duke had merely remarked, "I'll take damned good care he don't run away with me."

Diantha's first view of Wellington was at a ball. As it was for many others, her initial reaction was one of disappointment. He was neither tall nor splendidly dressed, and his frequent laughter had a slightly inane sound, like the braying of an ass. But when she waltzed with him she saw the ice-cold intelligence in the eyes over the beaky nose, and began to understand that the real Wellington lived behind the commonplace mask.

Shortly after their dance Diantha saw him gravitate toward a woman who had just entered. She was a luxurious, black-haired beauty, perhaps a little too voluptuous to be elegant, but superb in her wine red velvet dress, her throat and wrists flashing with rubies. She seemed to be in her late thirties, an age when many women had faded. But this creature evidently still considered herself in the prime of life, capable of conquering any man she wanted. And she was right, Diantha thought, watching Wellington's attentions with amusement.

She fanned herself, for the room was hot, and moved closer to where she could see Rex. He hadn't noticed her, but was scanning the dancers, perhaps looking for her. Diantha was about to approach him with a joke about being enough of a dowdy to dance with her own husband, when she froze, startled by a change that had come over him. Wellington and his partner had waltzed close to Rex, giving him a clear view of the gorgeous creature in the wine red dress. Diantha saw him go pale. The hand he'd been raising halted in midair, and a stillness settled over his whole frame that had something frightening in it.

Diantha went nearer until she was only a few feet away. If Rex had turned his head slightly, he would have been bound to see her, but he didn't move by so much as a fraction. All his attention was on the woman. He was watching her with blazing eyes, as if his whole fate depended on her.

The dance ended. Wellington noticed Rex and hailed him. With the woman on his arm he went across the floor, and Diantha clearly heard him say, "I believe this lady is an old friend of yours."

"Yes," Rex said. "Lady Bartlett and I . . . have met before."

Chapter Ten

Lady Bartlett!

The name rang like a death knell in Diantha's mind. This was the woman Rex had adored to the point of idolatry, who'd betrayed and mocked him, and left him a wounded half man, whose powers of love had withered.

Still unnoticed, she stood like a frozen statue, listening. Lady Bartlett gave Rex a slow, significant smile, implicit with shared memories. "Why, Rex," she murmured, "after all this time. How many years is it?"

"Eight years and four months," Rex answered, his face still pale.

"What a precise memory you have!" She chuckled, a rich, luxurious sound. "And how ungallant of you to recall the years so well."

Rex's face was livid. "I recall everything," he said with an effort.

Lady Bartlett held out her hand, palm down, leaving Rex no choice but to carry it to his lips. Diantha had a perfect view of her face, the lips smiling in triumph, the eyes gleaming with a strange light. Then Rex raised his head and her face changed, becoming again the perfect social mask.

"I trust your husband is well," Rex said politely.

"Poor James died four years ago."

Rex's face was white. "That must be a sad loss to you."

He became aware of Diantha standing near and beckoned to her. "My dear, I should like to introduce you to Lady Bartlett, an old acquaintance of mine. Lady Bartlett, my wife."

"How do you do, Lady Chartridge." Rex's onetime love regarded her with a piercing glance. "It's a pleasure to meet you at last. I've heard so very much about you."

"I wonder what you can possibly have heard of interest," Diantha said coolly.

Lady Bartlett laughed. "Why, in this frantic little society of ours, no one has secrets. May I present my brother Anthony, Lieutenant Hendrick."

She indicated a swaggering, handsome lad who'd appeared nearby. He had blue-black hair and a good-looking face that had something stupid and disagreeable about it. He raised Diantha's hand to his lips, holding it just too long for propriety.

"Don't you love that waltz?" Lady Bartlett asked as the band struck up again. "Dance with me for old times' sake, Rex."

He bowed and led her onto the floor. The Duke of Wellington had departed in search of other prey, and Diantha was left alone with Anthony Hendrick. He gave her an elaborate bow.

"Your humble servant, Lady Chartridge. Dare I beg the honor of a dance, or am I being too forward?"

Despite his protestations of humility, his whole being radiated confidence in his masculine attractions. A faint sneer seemed permanently fixed onto his lips. Diantha had seldom disliked anyone so much at first glance, but she nodded and took his hand.

She waltzed mechanically. With every fiber of her

being she was aware of Rex and Lady Bartlett whirling about the room. She knew when the voluptuous creature laughed, glancing up into Rex's face from beneath lowered lids. His own expression was tense and hard, the look of a man rigidly suppressing his feelings. But what feelings? The question filled Diantha with turmoil, until her head ached.

"I beg your pardon?" She came out of her reverie to realize that Hendrick was talking.

"Just my luck," he said, "to be talking to the most beautiful woman in the room, but she ain't listening."

"I've heard of your sister as a great beauty," Diantha responded politely. "And now I see it's true."

"Oh yes, the men fall over Ginevra," he said carelessly. "Always have. Dashed useful to have that kind of a sister." He gave a self-satisfied smirk.

"Indeed it must be," she replied in a colorless tone.

"You should have seen her when she was younger. They called her a goddess. How she used to laugh! Funny how they always came back for more. Once she had her claws into them, she never let go. I say, are you all right?"

"I'm a little faint," she said, swaying. "Please, help me from the floor."

"Shall I fetch your husband?"

"On no account in the world. I wish for no fuss."

She let him help her to a chair and fetch her a drink, praying that she wouldn't attract attention. It wasn't the first dizzy spell she'd had recently, and she was becoming more certain of their meaning. She'd planned to tell Rex as soon as she was sure, but now . . .

She closed her eyes as her head swam again.

When she opened them Hendrick was there with her drink.

"Thank you," she said. "Be so good as to leave me now. It will soon be suppertime, and you'll want to take one of the Misses Sedgewick in. They're all the rage."

He trotted away in search of a supper companion while Diantha drank the cold cordial. As soon as she was strong enough she forced herself to her feet, fixed a smile on her face, and allowed an elderly general to take her in to supper.

When it was time to return to the ballroom she watched anxiously for Rex and Lady Bartlett, but there was no sign of them. The next moment she jumped as, from close behind her, she heard a woman's voice, rich and husky, vibrant with invitation.

"Our meeting wasn't an accident, Rex—I knew you'd be here."

Then Rex, speaking too quietly for Diantha to hear the words. She turned and found a heavy brocade curtain shielding the two who were talking. But from behind it Lady Bartlett's voice came again.

"It wasn't easy to come by news, living in exile as I've been. First I was kept out of society by the scandal, and then, when I'd worked my way back a little, I didn't have any money. It's been a terrible life, but I've always known what happened to you. I made it my business to know. Do you remember when—?"

Somebody squeezed past. Diantha had to move. She could just make out the murmur of Rex's voice, then a sudden burst of laughter from his companion. "Oh, come, my dear Rex, I think I know you better than that—"

Every inch of Diantha's body ached with the strain of trying to hear. She was in torment, longing to escape, but needing to know everything that was said.

Lady Bartlett was talking again. "I was fascinated to hear you'd married Miss Halstow. I wonder if you know why . . . Yes, of course you do. . . ."

Diantha stood rigid at the mention of her own name. Her heart was thundering. If only she could hear what Rex replied, but his words were muffled. Only the tone reached her, intense, feverish. Then a few clear words, ". . . can't talk to you here . . ."

"No, it's too public," Lady Bartlett agreed. "We must meet somewhere private, where we can be sure of not being disturbed. . . . So much to say to you . . . dance with me again. . . ."

This time Rex's voice reached Diantha clearly. It was fierce and full of some intense emotion. "I don't trust myself to dance with you. . . ."

Diantha edged away, feeling that she would scream if she heard any more. The whole room seemed part of a bad dream that whirled around her.

George and Elinor were ready to leave. They never remained long at parties, attending only out of politeness and always eager to return home to be alone together. Usually they sent the carriage back for the others.

"I think I'll leave with you tonight," Diantha said, affecting a yawn. "I'm vastly tired."

"Will Rex come, too?" Elinor asked.

Diantha smiled brightly. "I'm sure he will, if I can only find him."

At last she saw her husband making his way through the crowd. He was still dreadfully pale, but he forced a smile when he saw her.

"We're leaving," she told him. "Do you come?"

"I think I'll stay awhile, m'dear."

"Perhaps I ought to stay with you," she said, determinedly cheerful, although her heart was thumping painfully.

"Not at all." He kissed her cheek. "Go home to bed. If you don't get some rest soon, your dissipations will exhaust you."

"Do you think you'll be late?" She knew the question was unwise, and Rex's coolly raised eyebrows confirmed it.

"I may be," he said. "Don't wait up for me."

Diantha was forced to take a deep breath to steady herself. She wanted to throw her arms around him and drag him bodily to the carriage, anything to prevent him remaining here with Lady Bartlett. Instead she smiled and departed with the others.

In the carriage on the way home Elinor said, "It's not like Rex to stay without you."

"We don't interfere with each other's amusements," Diantha said, trying to speak calmly.

"I know. I only meant—" Feeling her husband's warning pressure on her hand, Elinor stopped. "Perhaps he wants to play cards," she said lamely.

Mercifully they soon reached the house. Diantha retired immediately, glad to be alone with her shattering emotions. Nothing in her life had prepared her for the violence of feeling that shook her now. Rex had loved that woman, worshiped her, and her reappearance had devastated him. His face had left no doubt of that. He'd stayed behind to be private with her. Diantha buried her face in her hands, wondering what they were doing now.

She went to bed, but couldn't sleep. Where was he? Was Lady Bartlett in his arms, receiving the suffocating kisses of passion that she'd thought were hers alone? The night stretched ahead of her, full of torment.

At last she fell into a restless doze. She awoke

with a start to find that it was six in the morning. Rising stiffly, she went to the door that connected her room to Rex's. Hearing nothing from the other side, she softly turned the handle and looked in.

The pale gray light of dawn showed that the room was empty and the bed undisturbed.

The round of balls, parties, and picnics intensified. Lady Chartridge threw several splendid soirees and receptions, one of which was graced by Belgian royalty. In the whirl of organizing it was possible to pretend that she hadn't heard the rumors. Rex had taken Lady Bartlett driving, and introduced her to various friends and their wives. He was also often to be seen in the company of Anthony Hendrick, a crass, vulgar young man whom nobody else liked.

At least, she thought, she hadn't needed to behave like other neglected wives and sit at home weeping. Her own mantelpiece was jammed with cards of invitation, and she accepted them all. No one was so merry as Lady Chartridge. No one went to so many balls, picnics, excursions. No one danced with so many men or broke so many of their hearts. And no one was so lonely, desolate, and bewildered.

"The devil of it is that Hendrick's been appointed as an aide to General Picton," Bertie said one day. "Picton's mad as fire, but he can't do anything about it. Someone's been pulling strings higher up."

"Do you know who that 'someone' might be?" Diantha asked, bent over the menu she was altering.

"I did hear a rumor that it was Rex, but dash it all, it can't be! He knows what a fool Hendrick is. He's got too much sense to force him on us—ain't he?"

"I know nothing of military matters," Diantha said with a shrug.

"Neither do I," Bertie said frankly. "But you don't need to be a military genius to know that you're better off without a fellow like that."

"Well, it probably wasn't Rex at all," Diantha observed. "It may have been the duke himself. I believe he greatly admires Lady Bartlett."

"Wellington admires a lot of beauties," Bertie said, "but he don't give military office to their idiot relatives. The story is that she tried it and Wellington snubbed her. Could it have been Rex, d'you think?"

"I haven't the slightest idea," Diantha said coldly.

Beneath her calm surface she was in a turmoil of misery. Her heart knew that it was true. There was nothing Rex wouldn't do for this woman.

"Luckily Picton's got his measure," Bertie went on. "He won't give him anything important to do. He takes simple messages here and there, and apart from that he sits around giving himself airs." He looked up as Rex appeared in the doorway. "I was talking about Picton's new errand boy, Hendrick," he said angrily.

Rex shrugged. "Why waste your breath? A stupid young man. But I believe he bows nicely and looks good on parade, and that is all his job requires."

Bertie shrugged and took himself off.

"Hard at work for your reception?" Rex inquired pleasantly.

"Yes, the invitations went out two days ago, and they've all been accepted," Diantha replied.

"I believe you sent no invitation to Lady Bartlett," Rex said quietly.

"True." Diantha's heart began to hammer.

"Did you have some reason for omitting her?" Rex asked in the same soft voice.

"I had no reason to include her. I barely know her."

"But she is an old friend of mine. You failed to include her in your last soiree, and I would be grateful if this time you would send her a card."

Diantha stiffened. "I do not like Lady Bartlett," she said tensely.

"My dear, since when was it necessary to like all your guests? If I ask you to do me this favor, can you not agree for my sake?"

Diantha rose abruptly and began to walk about the room, needing the release of movement. "Isn't it enough that you make a public scandal with her?" she demanded.

"Nonsense!" Rex said in the hardest voice he'd ever used toward her. "Don't exaggerate, Diantha. There's been no public scandal. I've driven with her and danced with her. What of that? You went driving with Sinclair yesterday, and were away a devilish long time. Did I kick up a dust?"

"No, you cared nothing," she said in a flat voice.

"Precisely. That is the way a sensible man behaves. And your other admirers, who clutter this house with their posies and gifts. Beyond asking you to move them so that I can get into my own hallway, have I raised objections?"

"None," she sighed.

"Then why all this fuss because I ask you to invite an old friend?"

"Perhaps because she's an older friend than you tell me?"

His face was cold. "What do you mean by that?"

Pride, and her promise to George, made it impossible to confront him with everything she knew. Instead she said, "I mean that you never mentioned her until she arrived in Brussels, and the sight of her made you look like a ghost."

"Come, come, we don't need to indulge in melodramatics, do we? Look like a ghost!"

"You didn't see your own face when she appeared," Diantha cried.

"I can well believe I showed astonishment. It was so long since I'd seen her. Anything more was your imagination."

She longed to believe him, but there was an air of tension about him that she couldn't mistake. He was deceiving her, hoping she would probe no further. But some little inner demon forced her to go on tormenting herself.

"I think she means far more to you than you pretend," she said.

"And why should you think that?"

"Because I've never known you like this before."

She raised her eyes to his face and saw there a look of hauteur that almost made her quail. "Perhaps," Rex said after a moment, "but then neither of us really knows the other well, do we? I seem to recall that we had a bargain to keep our hearts and minds in our own care, and not ask each other impertinent questions."

If he'd slapped her, it wouldn't have hurt more than that casual word "impertinent." She'd seen Rex angry, but never before had he snubbed her with this bleak, wintry finality. Her temper rose. How dared he expect her to invite his fancy woman to her home!

"You don't know what you're asking," she said flatly. "My other guests would not expect to meet Lady Bartlett."

"It's true she's not invited out as often as you are yourself," he said. "But she's gradually gaining acceptance, and an invitation from you would help her greatly. Kindly send her a card."

"And have everyone staring at me and wondering

if I know that you got her brother onto Picton's staff?" she cried.

She saw him flinch, and her heart died a little as she realized that the stories were true.

"Listening to backstairs gossip, Diantha?" he demanded satirically.

"Do you deny it? *Can* you?"

"No, I don't deny it. Why should I? I'm not ashamed of helping an old friend."

"Anthony Hendrick is a good-for-nothing puppy, the sort of man you wouldn't waste five minutes on unless—"

"Unless what? Be careful, Diantha. What I do for my friends is my business." His voice softened slightly. "Come," he said with an echo of his old kindness. "Why make a fuss over a trifle? Try not to think the worst of me, Diantha. Believe me, I don't deserve it."

"Then why have you changed since she came to Brussels?"

"That—I cannot tell you."

But she knew, she thought, looking at him in anguish. Her chin set. He needn't think he could delude her by using the old, kindly tone.

"If you refuse to tell me, what can I do but think the worst?" she asked stubbornly. "You once promised me fidelity—"

"And I've kept my word."

"Have you? When suddenly you're away from home night after night, and Brussels seethes with tales of how you are constantly in her company?"

"If you and I had married for love," he said slowly, "I might really have asked you to look into your heart and trust me. But what should two people like us do, stranded without love to help them?"

"Rex, what is this woman to you?"

The softness left his face. "A touch too possessive,

my dear. One might almost think you were a jealous wife. Surely this is exactly the kind of scene we once promised ourselves not to indulge in? I've given you my word that I'm faithful, and I don't expect to be questioned further. What I do expect is that you send Lady Bartlett a card for your reception. Will you oblige me in this?"

"I will not."

He gave her a colder look than she'd ever had from him before, and walked out without another word.

The Duke of Wellington had promised to be present at Lady Chartridge's ball. So had Prince William of the Belgian royal family. Some of the highest ranks of the army would also be there, Lieutenant General Sir Rowland Hill, known as "Daddy Hill" for his easygoing manner, Lord Uxbridge, Sir Hussey Vivian: all of them invested with an aura of glamour. By now everyone knew that Wellington was going into battle with half his best men unavailable because they'd been sent to fight in America. His army was a motley crowd of English, Belgians, Dutch, and Hanoverians. Many of them were excellent fighters, but they weren't used to each other, and they all had their own weapons and ammunition. The fate of Europe depended on these men, fighting a united French army who worshiped Bonaparte and thought he couldn't lose. So their commanders were sought after at social events.

Before the evening began Diantha had a quiet word with Hector, her steward.

"If Lady Bartlett appears, she is not to be admitted," she said firmly. "Tell the footmen that no one—no one at all—is to be allowed in without a card."

"Very good, my lady."

Then she was standing in the reception line, with Rex by her side. Wellington arrived early, bent low over her hand, and claimed a waltz. But then he sought out some of his officers and plunged into a discussion.

The musicians she had hired were the best. Diantha knew that no one could find fault with the supper she had laid out, or the quality of the wines. As the stream of guests arrived Diantha began to relax, feeling that the evening was going well.

"I think Hector wants to speak to you," Elinor said.

Diantha saw her steward discreetly trying to attract her attention and beckoned him over. He looked troubled.

"Lady Bartlett has arrived, my lady," he murmured.

"You have your orders."

"But, my lady, she has a card of invitation."

"That's impossible!" she said fiercely.

Then she saw Rex looking at her and read the truth in his eyes. "How dare you do this!" she breathed softly.

"Very well, Hector," Rex said to the steward. "Show Lady Bartlett in." Diantha whirled and faced him. "Don't reveal that you're upset," he murmured. "People will be watching. They must see you welcome her."

"I'll die first."

"You'll die socially if you insult your guest. Think what people will say of you, and use your splendid common sense."

"I will never forgive you for this!" she flashed. "Never!"

Rex didn't answer. His eyes had gone past her to the woman who had appeared in the doorway. She was wearing deep blue velvet that accentuated the blue-black of her luxuriantly curled hair. Her head was up as if in defiance, and her brilliant eyes swept around her, coming to rest on Rex.

For a moment it seemed as if the whole room was silent, electrified by tension. Then Rex left his wife's side, crossed to Ginevra Bartlett, and raised her hand to his lips.

Years of strict rearing came to Diantha's aid, enabling her to walk across to her new guest with a smile on her face hiding the misery in her heart.

"I'm so glad you were able to accept my invitation," she said. "I feared that something might prevent you."

"I would have allowed nothing to prevent me," Lady Bartlett replied sweetly. "An invitation from Lady Chartridge is an honor for which I had hardly dared to hope."

Diantha looked her steadily in the eye. "Any friend of my husband's, madam, is a friend of my own."

"How kind you are. I had hoped that we might be friends. Perhaps later in the evening we could—"

"There'll be time enough for talking," Rex interrupted. "Dance with me, Jenny. This is my favorite waltz."

He seized her around the waist and swept her onto the dance floor. Diantha gripped her fan until her knuckles turned white. Was he so desperate to get that woman into his arms that he must adopt such blatant tactics?

But she was the hostess. None of this must appear in her face. So she smiled and danced with the Duke of Wellington, then Sir Hussey Vivian, and after him the Prince of Orange. She laughed at their sallies, accepted their compliments on the success of the evening, so that no one would suspect that she was aware of her husband every moment. She knew that he never left Ginevra Bartlett's side. Sometimes he danced with her himself, other times he watched while she danced, and claimed her company again the moment she was free. He took her in to supper, her arm drawn through his own, and Diantha smiled and smiled, knowing that the other guests were watching her.

When supper was over and they all returned to the ballroom Rex was still at her elbow, but she waved him away to take the duke's arm. Diantha saw how Rex's eyes followed every move she made, and she felt as if her heart would break.

When the dance had finished she began to approach Lady Bartlett, who turned as she saw her coming. For a moment it seemed as if the two women would speak, but Rex intervened, drawing Ginevra away to introduce her to someone.

"I can't think what Rex is about," George said, at her elbow. "Doesn't he know he's attracting comment? Not that there can be anything in it, of course," he added hastily. "But what on earth is he doing?"

"I can tell you what he's doing," Diantha said bitterly. "He's protecting her from me. He's afraid that I'll insult her."

"Does he know that I told you about her?"

"No. I promised you, and I'll keep my word."

"Perhaps you should break it," George said gently. "Then you two could speak frankly and clear the air."

"Thank you, dear George, but it's too late for that. I have eyes in my head. There are some things that can't be explained."

"Would you like me to tell him that you know—?"

"No," she said swiftly. "There are things—I can't explain—but you must leave this to us."

At last the dreadful evening was over. Diantha bid her guests farewell with an aching head. There was no sign of Rex when she was finally free to retire to her room. When she was undressed she dismissed Eldon and threw herself across the bed, wondering how she was going to endure life.

She laid her hands over her stomach. Somehow she must endure, for the sake of the precious life she carried. She thought of how it might have been, how she would once have enjoyed sharing her secret with Rex. But how could she tell him now? What would it mean to him? Perhaps nothing now he was reunited with his true love. At last, the fierce self-control that had supported her all evening broke down, and she wept brokenheartedly into her pillow.

She awoke in the last minutes of darkness before dawn. Her mouth was dry. She remembered that there was some cordial in the library, and it seemed easier to go for it herself than ring for a maid. Slipping on a dressing gown, she crept down the stairs.

In the library she saw a pair of long legs protruding from deep within a wing chair. Investigating further, she discovered Bertie, still dressed as he had been for the reception, except that now he was in his shirtsleeves, and his shirt was torn open at the neck.

But he was not, as he would once have been, slumped comotose beside an empty brandy decanter. The decanter was almost full, and Bertie was awake, clear-eyed and staring into space. He started when he saw Diantha and forced a smile.

"So this is where you disappeared to, you wretch," she chided him, sitting down in a chair near him.

"Your party was too exciting for me," he said.

"Why don't you go to bed?"

"I've been meaning to for hours, but somehow—I just can't be bothered to get up and climb the stairs."

"I could send your man to carry you to bed," Diantha said lightly. "I'm sure he's done so often before."

"Ah yes, at one time. Not now. I couldn't make myself touch that decanter. *She* didn't like me to drink. It's strange that I'm trying to be the man she wanted now, when she isn't here to know, when I'll probably never see her again—"

"No," Diantha said softly. "It isn't strange." She sighed. "Go to bed, Bertie."

"I will in a minute. Leave me alone for a while."

She kissed his cheek gently and left the room. From the street outside she could hear the sound of carriage wheels, and wondered who was traveling at this early hour. She paused, alert, when she heard the wheels stop outside her own house. The next moment the porter was opening the door.

Two people stood on the step outside. Diantha's hands flew to her face as she saw who they were. The elder of the two stepped forward and spoke quietly.

"We must ask your pardon, Lady Chartridge, for coming here without warning, and at this unseasonable hour—"

He got no further. Diantha backed into the library, her eyes fixed on her visitors in joyous disbelief.

"Bertie," she said urgently. "Bertie, *get up and look who's here.*"

He rose and stared at the door. The next moment Sophie ran forward with a cry of gladness and was crushed in his arms.

Chapter Eleven

Sophie and Bertie were married two days later. The Reverend Dunsford assisted the local pastor and watched tenderly as his daughter gave her hand to the man she loved.

"She was grief-stricken without him," he'd told Diantha as they waited to leave for the wedding. "I tried to persuade myself that it would pass, that she would find a better husband, a man of stern moral character. But," he sighed, "this is the man her heart has chosen, and I am a father as well as a clergyman. I could not stand by and watch her misery, especially when we heard that he had joined the army. Despite everything that has happened, I believe there is much good in him. So I told her I would bring her here."

"I'm sure you did the right thing," Diantha assured him. "Bertie has changed more than I would have believed possible." She smiled. "He never goes out to enjoy himself, and he sat all night with a full brandy bottle, refusing to touch it because Sophie wouldn't like it. She's become his lodestar. He'd do anything to please her. He may yet finish up in holy orders."

"I'm saying nothing to him on the subject. If he comes to that, it must be for the right reasons. And if they love each other, perhaps that's all that matters."

Diantha gave a little sigh. "Yes," she said. "That's all that matters."

Now here she was at their wedding, watching Sophie come down the aisle on Rex's arm, smiling for Bertie. When the time came for him to slip the ring on her finger their faces glowed with their mutual joy.

There was a pain in Diantha's heart. This was how a wedding ought to be. She had thought herself so clever, marrying in a mood of cool calculation. But she hadn't been clever at all. She'd been stupid and ignorant beyond belief, and she was paying the price for it now.

She wondered what was going through Rex's mind, and looked up to find him watching her. Since the night of the ball they'd barely spoken. For a moment she wanted to reach out to him, but the memory of his behavior that night stood between them. She looked quickly away. That was how things were between them now. Perhaps it was how they would always be.

Anyone who was anyone had been invited to the Duchess of Richmond's ball on June 15. Ambassadors, royalty, aristocracy, all would congregate in the vast mansion in the Rue de la Blanchisserie. Wellington's officers would be there, too, and the great man himself. He'd personally assured the duchess that nothing would interrupt her ball. Some of those who hung on his words took this as a sign that Wellington didn't expect Bonaparte to make a move. Others, perhaps more discerning, wondered if the duke was trying to prevent a panic.

Certainly by the morning of the fifteenth the city was alive with reports that the Belgian/French border had been sealed off. Rumors flew that the French army was on the march. But from which direction? Nobody knew. Until he received definite news of his enemy's whereabouts, Wellington could make no move. So he dressed for the evening, with an air of supreme unconcern.

"How can he go to a ball when the French may be marching on us?" Elinor asked.

"It's the best place for him to be," George told her. "All his highest officers will be there. If he receives any news, he's got them to hand." He kissed his wife. "Now, we're going to forget such things and enjoy ourselves."

Diantha's dress was Madame Fillon's masterpiece, a dazzling creation of cream satin embroidered with seed pearls. The bosom was cut so low that Madame had queried it. None of the other evening gowns she'd made for Lady Chartridge had been nearly so daring. But her ladyship had confirmed it, with a strange blazing look in her eyes that Madame had never seen there before.

Elinor came into Diantha's room, quietly elegant in blue silk. She stopped as she saw the neckline, but before she could say anything she met Diantha's eyes in the mirror. Like Madame Fillon, she was shocked at something reckless in them. This was Diantha as she'd never known her before, but it seemed all of a piece with the strange mood her cousin had been in recently.

Eldon appeared with the Chartridge pearls and began to attire her mistress with the tiara, the necklace, and the bracelet.

"How lovely they are," Elinor sighed. "I remember how you exclaimed over them when Rex gave them to you, and how beautiful you looked wearing them at your wedding."

Diantha had been holding up her wrist, turning it to examine the jewels, but at this she stopped as if frozen.

"My wedding," she repeated in a dreamlike voice. "Yes, I wore them at my wedding."

The next moment she'd stripped the bracelet from her wrist and tossed it onto the dressing table. A swift movement tore the tiara from her hair. "Take it off," she commanded Eldon, pointing to the necklace.

"But, Diantha," Elinor protested, "they're beautiful."

"I want them off." Diantha took a breath to calm herself. "I'll wear my diamonds instead."

Eldon was impassive as she removed the last of the pearls and put them away. She was too well trained to betray surprise, and besides, she'd grown used to Lady Chartridge's strange moods recently. She brought out the diamonds, and soon Diantha's neck, ears, and arms were glittering. Last of all was the diamond aigrette in her shining golden hair, and she was ready.

She looked magnificent, Elinor thought. Every inch a countess. But somehow she liked her less well this way. Before they came to Brussels she'd sensed a softening in Diantha, as though she'd discovered peace and happiness. But if so, they'd deserted her, leaving this brilliant, unapproachable creature.

Bertie, who hadn't been invited, saw them off without regret. His idea of pleasure now was an evening at home with Sophie, for who knew how many more they would have? The Reverend Dunsford had returned to England, content to leave his daughter with the man who loved her.

From the moment they arrived they could all feel the electric tension in the Richmonds' mansion. Something was going to happen tonight, and everyone knew it. Beneath the glorious display, the dress uniforms, brave with silver and gold lace, beneath the satins and silks, diamonds and pearls, lay the reality of a war machine lumbering slowly but inexorably into life. Many of those who danced most merrily tonight would never see another ball. Among the young girls were some who were wearing colors for the last time in their lives.

The great ballroom had been covered in rose trellis paper, and hung with tentlike draperies in gold, crimson, and black. Flowers and ribbons wreathed the pillars, and a multitude of chandeliers filled the ballroom with light.

As Diantha entered on Rex's arm she quickly scanned the throng for a sight of Lady Bartlett, but there was no sign of her. But her relief was short-lived, when a glance at Rex revealed that he was doing the same. She thought she saw a change come over his frame, but in her distraught state she didn't know how to understand it. Was he relieved not to see her, or anxious lest she didn't arrive?

The music was playing. Young men, some in uniform, some not, crowded around Diantha, begging for dances. It was like the early days of her marriage again, and yet unlike, for then she'd been an ignorant girl who'd thought hearts could be played with. She knew better now that her own heart was breaking.

When the evening was in full swing the duke arrived. He was dressed with his usual neatness and elegance and appeared unconcerned. One daring young lady ran up to him to ask if the rumors of battle were true, and he replied composedly, "Yes, they are true. We are off tomorrow."

Men and women looked at each other, knowing that the hectic life they had been leading for the last few months was over. These were its last moments.

Diantha watched for any sign of the duke talking urgently to his generals, but he seemed untroubled.

"Why isn't he giving orders or something?" she asked.

"He's waiting for more information," George told her. "Most of his army is concentrated in the north, because he's convinced Bonaparte will attack from there and cut him off from the sea. General Blucher and the Prussian army are in the south, near Ligny. Either one of them can move to join the other, depending on where Boney attacks. But at the moment there's no way of knowing."

There was a pause in the dancing. Sixteen young Scotsmen in swinging kilts took the floor for a display of Highland dancing. When they had finished the girls threw flowers that cascaded over the young men as they marched off the floor.

Diantha, applauding with the rest, suddenly saw Lady Bartlett standing with Rex. They were talking, their heads close together. Diantha couldn't make out the words, but she could sense Rex's urgency. His words poured out quickly, and he made sharp movements with his hand. Lady Bartlett shook her beautiful head, and Rex's manner became more intense, more insistent. With a dreadful sense of shock Diantha realized that her husband was pleading with this woman.

For a moment the hot blood ran to her head and she was on the verge of running across the floor to confront them, strike the painted creature across the face, anything to break up the scene. Then common sense intervened. She couldn't make a scene here. The next moment they had turned and left the room.

When it was time for supper she was gallanted by two men who vied for her attention. She laughed and flirted with them both, and tried not to wonder where Rex was, or if he was with that woman. The Duke of Wellington was similarly occupied, flirting with a lady on each side, and giving his inane laugh at their sallies, as though he had nothing better to do.

But during the first course a messenger appeared and spoke quietly to Wellington. The company saw the duke go still, fighting to control a look of outraged disbelief. He dismissed the messenger with orders to get some sleep, and applied himself again to his food.

But as soon as he could do so without hurry he left the supper table and strolled away with his host. Those left behind looked at each other, wondering what it all meant.

They were soon to learn. By the time dancing resumed the ballroom was alive with the news that Bonaparte had crossed the frontier.

"But why did he look so shocked?" Diantha asked of George. "It's what he must have been waiting for."

"But not like this," George said grimly. "The duke was sure Boney would attack his rear, and he's been fortifying the northwest accordingly. But Boney's come up from the south and got to within twenty miles of Brussels. Our army is concentrated in the wrong place. It will be hours before the troops can be got into position, and that will give Bonaparte time to—" He stopped, remembering that he was talking to ladies. "I must go," he said. "There's just time to change before I have to report for duty."

All about them people were drifting away, stealing a final kiss in the shadows, or hurrying off to go into action. Diantha looked around, not expecting to see Rex, but he was there, shouldering his way through the crowd.

"George is leaving," she told him.

"Then let us leave also," he said, his face grim. "There's nothing to stay for here."

In Brussels the night was alive. Wagons full of supplies and ammunition made a din on the cobbles as they rumbled to the Namur Gate to begin the journey south. Soldiers poured from the houses where they had been billeted.

Much of the noise took place directly under the windows of the house in the Rue Ducale. Inside, all was frantic preparation. George tore off his dress uniform and reappeared attired for duty. Elinor, very pale and silent, stayed with him until the last moment.

"Can you discuss your orders, or are they a secret?" Rex asked.

"We report to headquarters, then get to Quatre-Bras as fast as we can," George told him. "We won't stop Bonaparte there. Too many men are still in the north, and they can't travel fast enough. But we may hold him up while reinforcements arrive."

Bertie, too, was ready to go. Diantha saw Sophie take the gold cross from her neck, kiss it fervently, and put it around his neck.

"God will bring you back to me," she whispered. "He couldn't be so cruel as to part us now."

"I'm going to headquarters with them," Rex told Diantha. "I may learn some more news. Don't wait up for me."

The memory of him pleading with Lady Bartlett scorched across her brain. He was no longer hers, if, indeed, he had ever been hers.

"It was my intention to retire," she said coolly. "A safe journey."

They were at the door. The moment of parting was on them. The next moment the men had gone.

The women remained behind, silent in their distress.

By dawn the last soldiers had marched out of Brussels, and an ominous quiet fell over the city. The streets were no more alive with the various colors of uniforms. The laughing, swaggering young men had gone, some forever. That first day, the feelings of those who were left were confused. They knew that the fate of Europe hung on the battle to come, but their first thoughts were for the men who had marched away from them that morning.

Although Bertie's departure had left her distraught, Sophie recovered her calm quickly. Years of caring for people who were sick or troubled had made her strong.

"The wounded will be returning to Brussels soon after the fighting begins," she told Diantha and Elinor, "and we must be ready to help them. Madame Dellville is organizing a hospital. I mean to put myself at her disposal."

"An excellent plan," Diantha said. "We will all go."

Thankfully there was no time to think of her own heartache. The day was spent busily arranging for supplies to be taken to the hospital tent that was being erected at the Namur Gate of the city. Late in the afternoon their attention was arrested by a faint sound of thunder in the distance. It came again and again, and this time they knew. Not thunder. Cannon.

The three ladies dined alone. Rex was out seeking news, and late in the evening he returned, having spoken to friends at Allied Headquarters. The news was bad. Blucher and the Prussian army had been defeated by the French at Ligny.

"Wellington's troops engaged the French at

Quatre-Bras," Rex said. "As he expected, they managed to hold it, but no more. He's managing a strategic retreat now."

"You said they held it," Diantha reminded him.

"But Blucher was defeated and is in retreat. Wellington must retreat, too, to maintain their communications. He's falling back on Waterloo." He gave a hard laugh. "Do you remember the Highlanders who danced last night? Every one of them is dead."

The ladies were silent with horror. Elinor hid her face in her hands.

"George's regiment hasn't been engaged yet," Rex added, "so both he and Bertie are safe."

"And Lieutenant Hendrick?" Diantha asked coolly.

"Is also safe."

"What a relief for Lady Bartlett! I'm sure she's anxious for news."

Rex gave her a brief inclination of the head, and departed.

The news of the retreat spread like wildfire, and nervousness possessed the city. By the next morning several families had loaded their belongings onto wagons, ready for departure. Those who remained behind had their nerves shaken by the sight of a troop of Belgian cavalry galloping through the Namur Gate, shouting that the French were on their heels. No French appeared in pursuit, but the exodus became more hurried.

The sound of gunfire had ceased, but wagonloads of wounded had started to arrive, and Diantha, Elinor, and Sophie were kept busy. The tent was not yet ready, and injured men had to be tended in the streets. There was little that inexperienced nurses could do but offer water, which the men seized thankfully.

At last came the news that the tent was prepared, and almost at once the heavens opened. It became a struggle to get as many as possible under cover before they were drenched. After working for hours the three women returned home, wet and exhausted. That night Diantha stared out of her window, listening to the rain, thinking of the men trying to sleep out in the open, with the greatest battle of their lives still to come.

By next morning, mercifully, the rain had stopped. Rex came to the tent at the Namur Gate and worked with them until midday. Then, seeing the wounded beginning to pour in from the battle that had started, he took the chaise and drove into the Forest of Soignies, which lay between Brussels and Waterloo. The road was choked with carts of baggage and equipment on their way to the field, and men who had been wounded but who were still on their feet, limping painfully back to the city. He took as many of these as he could into the chaise, and turned back to Brussels.

He made several trips, and each time he learned a little more of what was happening.

"It's bad, isn't it?" Diantha asked, reading his face.

"I fear it is. Wellington is relying on Blucher to come to his aid, but the Prussians are so far away that it will be early evening before they can arrive. If they don't get there in time . . ." He left the implication hanging in the air.

"It doesn't seem possible," she breathed.

"I should have made you leave before this," he said. "Even now you could—"

"I won't leave without Sophie and Elinor, and they won't leave without their husbands," she said.

"And if Boney should march into Brussels?"

"Pooh! I'd just add him to my list of admirers. Do you think I couldn't?"

"I'm very sure you could. You're a brave woman, Diantha. Perhaps you should have been a soldier's wife." He added softly, "Or any man's wife but mine."

She met his gaze, unflinching. His eyes fell first.

"This isn't the time or place," he said, in the same quiet voice, "but soon I must talk to you. There are things that I—that you have to understand—"

"Diantha," Elinor was calling her. "We need some more lint."

"What were you going to say?" Diantha asked urgently.

"Not now." He gave a wry half smile. "I need time to get my courage to the sticking point first."

He moved aside to allow more wounded in, turned, and left the tent. Diantha watched his tall figure disappearing, wondering what he had to say that needed courage, relieved that it had been postponed, and calling herself a coward for her relief.

The day wore on, scorching hot. The direction of the wind meant that this time there was no sound of cannon, even though the battle was nearer. This silence from fighting that was barely ten miles away had an eerie quality. The soldiers who appeared, bleeding from frightful wounds, were like ghosts coming from hell.

With every man who came to the tent, each woman there would turn, fearful of seeing a loved face. If the face was that of a stranger, there would be a moment of relief, followed by more fear, lest he be lying dead. Those who could talk brought the latest news, and it was fearful. Blucher and the Prussians hadn't yet arrived, and the allied losses were terrible.

The light began to fade. The tent overflowed with wounded, and still they came. Hardly able to move from weariness, Diantha leaned down to wash away the grime from yet one more face. Only when the black was removed did she realize that this was someone she knew.

"Corporal Eston," she breathed. "George's regiment."

"Hallo, my lady," he whispered painfully. "What are you doing here? Not safe for ladies—you should go to the rear—"

"This isn't the battlefield," she told him. "You've been brought back to Brussels."

"What—Brussels? How—?"

"You must have been unconscious throughout the journey. Corporal, did you see my brother-in-law?"

"I should say! He saved me—got hurt—"

"George is hurt?" she echoed in horror.

"Shell got him—saw him fall—must have passed out then—"

"Oh God! But they would have brought him in, too, surely?"

"Not if he was d—" The corporal gave a groan and his eyes closed.

Careful not to attract Elinor's attention, Diantha found Sophie and told her what had happened. "We must search for him here," she said, "and if we don't find him—"

"Then he'll probably be on the next cart," Sophie said calmly. "Let us search at once." A painful tension was in her face. "Did the corporal say anything about Bertie?"

"Not a thing. That must be good news."

"I'm sure it is," Sophie said with a brave smile.

They went through the tent, finding those who wore dragoon uniforms. Then Diantha spoke to Lady Calhaven, who was taking down names and ranks of every arrival who could speak, but there was no trace of George's name. Two more carts arrived, but George wasn't on either of them.

"Oh God!" Diantha whispered. "He must still be out there."

"What has happened?" Elinor had noticed Diantha's distraught face. Now she read in it something that terrified her. "Tell me," she said, very pale. "I must know."

"George has been wounded," Diantha said. "We were trying to find him, but he's not here."

Elinor swayed and clutched the wall, but she didn't faint.

"He's probably at a dressing station on the field," Sophie said in her commonsense way.

Elinor raised tormented eyes to them. "Or lying dead," she whispered.

"No! Elinor, he's not dead," Diantha said, with a firmness she was far from feeling. "He can't be. He was wounded before and survived. Oh, thank God! There's Rex. *Rex*!"

He hurried over. "I've just delivered another load of poor devils," he said.

"Have you seen George?" Diantha demanded. "He's been wounded. We think he's still at Waterloo."

Rex drew a swift breath. "Who told you this?"

"Corporal Eston. He was brought in a few minutes ago."

"Did he say where on the field it happened?"

"He passed out before I could ask."

"I must speak to him."

But when they reached the pallet where the corporal had lain, a private infantry soldier was there.

"The man who was here before, where is he?" Diantha asked urgently.

"He died," the infantryman said hoarsely. "They took him away."

"Then I shall have to search over the whole field," Rex said.

The infantryman eyed him askance. "You going into that?" he demanded. "D'you know what it's like? A shell can get you as fast as any soldier."

"Nevertheless I shall go," Rex said firmly.

Out of sight, Diantha clenched her hands. Rex might be killed. She wanted to hold him back, beg him not to go. Then she pulled herself together. She knew he had to rescue his brother. And besides, her concern would mean nothing to him now.

"Let me go with you," Elinor begged him, white-faced.

"No, I'll do better alone," Rex said firmly. "Send a message home to be ready for George, and try not to worry."

He strode out of the tent. Impulsively Diantha ran after him. "Rex!" she called in agony.

He paused and looked back at her. "Yes, my dear?"

"Take care!"

"Are you worried about what that soldier said? Don't trouble your head. It'll be over by the time I get there."

"What were you going to say to me, before?"

He shook his head. "There's no time for that now. Don't fret. I'll return, and I'll bring George back with me."

He looked down into her face, distraught and pale with weariness. "Go home and get some rest," he said kindly.

He touched her cheek with a gentle finger, and was gone.

Chapter Twelve

The hours dragged past. The light faded. Surely the battle must be over now, but there was no definite news, only a steady stream of wounded and dying men, pouring into Brussels.

Diantha sent a message home that everything should be made ready for George, but there was no sign of him, or Rex. She, Sophie, and Elinor were all drooping with weariness, but none of them would leave the tent, knowing that when their men returned they would come through the Namur Gate first. They searched every cart that arrived, looking for familiar faces, anyone who could bring them news.

"Another cart," Diantha said, hearing the wheels on the cobbles. "Will it never end?" With weary steps the three of them went to the entrance of the tent.

"Diantha, look!" Elinor's voice was filled with urgency. She was holding up a lantern, and by its light they could just make out George's face. It was blackened and half-covered in blood from a wound in his head, and his eyes were closed.

"George, George," Elinor cried frantically, taking hold of his shoulders.

For a dreadful moment they thought he'd died in the cart, but then his eyes slowly opened so that he looked directly at his wife. A faint smile touched his strained face.

"Hallo," he whispered.

"Darling," she sobbed, "oh, my darling, are you badly hurt?"

"Nothing to speak of," he said weakly. "You can thank Bertie for that—saved my life—"

"Where is he?"

"Somewhere—back there—"

Searching among the other faces, all alike in their grime and desperation, they found Bertie. He was breathing, but he lay still, and no amount of calling seemed to revive him.

Men came from the tent and began to help the wounded down, to take them inside. Diantha summoned a footman she'd been using to run errands.

"Hurry home and tell them to send a carriage here quickly," she said. To Elinor she added, "When the doctor's seen them we'll nurse them at home."

She went and found Sophie, who'd just finished assisting at an operation. She looked gray and exhausted.

"Bertie's wounded," Diantha told her. "They're just bringing him in."

Sophie's hands flew to her face. Then she steadied herself and sped away. She found Bertie where he'd just been laid down. His eyes were still closed, and his left hand was clenched rigidly over the cross Sophie had given him.

"I can't examine him properly if I can't move his hand," said the surgeon.

Sophie leaned down and whispered in Bertie's ear. Then she touched his hand, which relaxed at once. The doctor examined him, grunting.

"Wounds in the shoulder and side," he pronounced at last. "He'll survive them if they're kept free of infection."

"I'll dress them," Sophie said at once.

George had also been wounded twice, once in the head and once in the leg. He was weak from loss of blood, but here, too, the doctor was optimistic if there was no infection. "Get him out of this place," he said, looking around him, "keep the wounds clean, and he should make it."

Elinor fell beside the bed in a passion of thankfulness. Diantha looked on, glad for Elinor and Sophie, but secretly a prey to mounting terror.

Then she felt a hand clutch desperately at her skirt and, glancing down, she saw Anthony Hendrick. He looked ghastly. One arm had been shot off at the shoulder, and his clothes were soaked with blood. "Help me," he whispered. "Help me."

"Diantha, the carriage is here," Elinor came to tell her. "The doctor says we can move them."

They helped the orderlies carry George and Bertie out to the chaise. The doctor was working on Hendrick, who cried out repeatedly. Diantha turned to go, but something held her back. She saw the doctor rise from tending Hendrick. He met her eyes and shook his head.

"Wait!" Diantha called to the orderlies. She indicated Hendrick. "Put him in the chaise, too."

They traveled slowly, so as not to jolt the injured men, and the journey seemed to take an age. Diantha looked into George's face, longing to ask him for news of Rex, but he'd slipped into unconsciousness.

At last they reached the house. Diantha's first task was to pen a brief note to Lady Bartlett, informing her of her brother's wounds, and where to find him. When it was dispatched she leaned back, wondering what had possessed her to behave as she had.

Lady Bartlett arrived within half an hour. She looked different from her usual self. She was dressed plainly, without face paint or perfume, and her beautiful face was haggard. Diantha received her politely but without warmth.

"I'll take you to your brother, madam," she said, and led the way upstairs.

Anthony Hendrick was lying very still, with his eyes open, staring vacantly. His sister gave a cry and dropped to her knees beside the bed. Diantha left them, and ordered refreshment to be sent up.

She slipped into George's room. He was awake and already had a healthier color, holding Elinor's hand in his, his eyes resting drowsily on her face.

"George," Diantha said intently, "Rex went to find you, some time ago."

"Never saw him," George whispered hoarsely. His throat was dry with gunpowder. "They must have brought me away before he got there."

"Were they still fighting when you left?"

He nodded. "But he'll be all right," he said. "Rex knows how to dodge a few bullets. And it's probably stopped by now."

But what could have happened in the last hour of fighting? Would she ever see her husband again?

She went down to find Lady Bartlett in the drawing room. She was sitting at a table, consuming a large brandy and staring into space.

"Your brother?" Diantha asked.

"He died a few minutes ago," Ginevra said vaguely. "Shock. Loss of blood." She pulled herself together with an effort. "Thank you for bringing him here."

Diantha made a gesture of disclaimer. "I was happy to do what I could to help you," she said formally.

Lady Bartlett looked at her. "That's not true," she said bluntly. "You hate me, don't you?"

Diantha didn't answer. It was true, but she couldn't speak of her hate in the face of such misery.

"You hate me," Ginevra went on. "But you have no cause. Don't you realize that?"

"Do you expect me to believe you," Diantha asked, "when with my own ears I heard you say you'd come to Brussels to find my husband?"

"Yes, I did say that. But do you know why I came?"

"I can imagine."

"Lord, but you're a fool!"

Diantha stared, shocked as much by the forceful tone as by the words.

"You're a fool, Lady Chartridge, because you can't see what's under your nose. Your husband loves you. I hadn't been here five minutes before he made that very plain to me. And I was glad. Yes, glad. Because it gave me a hold over him I wouldn't otherwise have had."

"A hold? You mean you—?"

"Yes, I've been blackmailing him." Ginevra gave a hard laugh. "Not a pretty word, but then, I'm not a pretty character. I've lived on the fringes of society ever since my husband killed my lover in a duel, and I had to find a way back. Not for my own sake, but for the sake of my brother, the only person in the world that I ever really loved.

"There was nothing I wouldn't do for him, even blackmail. I forced your husband to get him a good army post. And I forced him to help me back into society, because there I could be most useful to Anthony. Rex hated it. He dislikes and despises me, but he had to give in to me, because I had one threat to hold over his head."

"I don't understand," Diantha said. "What could you blackmail him with? That old affair between you? Surely—"

"No, of course not. It wasn't even an affair. He was an innocent boy, and far too gentlemanly. No, it's something much more dangerous." She searched Diantha's pale face. "You really don't know, do you?"

"No, tell me."

"I threatened to tell you the name of my lover, the one who died at my husband's hand. Rex would do anything to prevent that. He said you idolized him."

"Him—who?"

"Why, Blair Halstow, of course. Your father."

"My—? I don't believe it," Diantha whispered.

Despite her words, her heart knew at once that this was true. It explained everything: the mystery of her father's death, Rex's anger at her tender memories of Blair. She sat down, trying desperately to come to terms with this shattering discovery.

Ginevra watched her for a moment, then filled another glass from the brandy decanter and handed it to her. Diantha drank it automatically.

"The night of your ball," Lady Bartlett said, "Rex stayed near me because he was afraid of what I might say. He didn't need to. I wasn't going to throw away my trump card when it was working so well, but his only thought was to protect you. He told me if I said a word to hurt you, he'd make me regret it all my days. He meant it, too. I didn't care as long as Anthony was advanced. When he was appointed to Picton's staff I was so proud, and now—"

Her whole body shook with grief. She laid her head on the table and sobbed uncontrollably. Full of pity, Diantha ventured to touch her shoulder.

After a moment Ginevra sat up and mopped her eyes. "It was generous of you to take him in, considering how you feel about me. Well, I can be generous, too. You're a very lucky woman, Lady Chartridge. There's nothing Rex wouldn't do to save you from pain. He loves you more than anything in the world. I'm sorry if the truth about your father hurts you, but it's better this way than for you to think Rex faithless."

"My father?" she echoed, dazed. "Hurt me—?"

Perhaps it should have hurt, but it didn't, she realized. How far away Blair seemed now! All that mattered was Rex. He loved her. As the mists of confusion cleared that blazing fact stood out, lighting the sky.

But Rex had gone to the battlefield. He was somewhere in that bloody chaos. He might be lying dead now.

She got to her feet, renewed strength flowing through her limbs. "I have to leave you," she said. She ran out of the salon without waiting for an answer.

On her way to her room she encountered Cranning, Rex's valet. "Where does your master keep his guns?" she asked swiftly.

"My lady—"

"Quickly. I must go to Waterloo and find him. I'll need a weapon."

The elderly man's face set. "You'll not go alone, my lady. His lordship would never forgive me. Leave it to me to get guns for both of us."

She nodded. In her room she threw off her clothes and donned riding dress. In a few minutes she was running down the stairs. Ginevra was standing in the hall.

"I've made arrangements for Anthony's body to be removed, Lady Chartridge," she said. "When you return we'll both be gone. Neither you nor your husband will ever hear of me again. God bless you, and keep you safe where you're going."

Impulsively Diantha kissed her. Then she hurried out to the stables. Cranning was already there with two saddled horses, and several wicked-looking pistols stuck into his belt. He quickly demonstrated one of these to Diantha.

"They'll try to steal the horses," he said briefly. "Shoot if you have to, or they'll shoot you." Doubt clouded his face. "It would be better if I went alone—"

"No!" she said fiercely. "I have to go. I have to find him. Even now it may be too late—" She stopped there. She wouldn't think of that, lest her courage fail.

The panic swirled around them as soon as they were out in the streets. The city thrummed with rumors: the battle was lost, Bonaparte was advancing on Brussels. People poured from houses to escape in any way they could. Loaded wagons stood useless with no animals to pull them. Fights broke out over the few nags available.

All around Diantha and Cranning eyes lit up at the sight of two fresh, well-fed horses. Men reached out frenzied hands to seize the bridles, but fell away as they saw the gleam of pistols. Diantha had begun by wondering if she could ever bring herself to use her weapon, but after the first few minutes she kept it cocked and at the ready. To her relief she found that by pointing it directly at someone's head, she could force him back.

And if I have to use it, I will, she thought grimly. *Nobody is going to stop me finding Rex. Oh, God, let him be alive!*

Somehow they forced a way through the streets until at last the Namur Gate came into sight. Then they were through it and heading for the Forest of Soignies. Here matters were even worse. The road through the forest was clogged with wagons that had overturned. Soldiers were on their way back from the battlefield, some riding as fast as they could through the chaos, others dragging themselves wearily. She stopped some of them, begging for news of the battle, but few knew anything except that it was over.

"It's finished," one man screamed at her. "They're all dead—all dead—"

Her common sense told her that it was impossible for everyone to be dead, but still the words chilled her. *All dead! All dead!* They tolled somberly through her weary mind. Rex might be dead, without knowing that his wife loved him and that they were to have a child.

Through the gathering darkness it was hard to tell what was ahead of her, but she thought she could see points of light. They seemed to be in pairs, and with a start of fear she discovered that she'd been surrounded by men. Someone cried, "Horses!" and the next moment hands were on her bridle, on her. She screamed and aimed her pistol, but she was pulled to the ground. A man dropped down beside her, but she fired. He howled and clapped a hand to his ear.

"Come on," said a disembodied voice in the darkness. "We've got the nags."

"No!" she cried, but a blow sent her flying backward. Her head sang, but she forced herself to sit up, discovering with relief that she still had the gun.

"Cranning!" she called.

"Oh, my lady, the horses!" he sobbed.

"Never mind. We'll go on foot."

They helped each other up and stumbled forward. All around them was a howling wilderness. Once the moon appeared from behind a cloud, showing her a scene of desolation. Men sat weeping beside overturned carts, either too injured or too exhausted to go further. There were other women on the road, evidently on the same errand as herself. Most were traveling toward the battlefield, but some were on their way back, supporting injured men, or alone, walking slowly, their eyes stunned.

One woman was screaming as she made her way toward Brussels, holding a wrapped bundle in her arms. "No," she howled, "no, my husband isn't dead. *He isn't dead.* He isn't, he isn't."

She placed herself in front of Diantha. *"He isn't dead."*

"I'm—glad," Diantha said, trying to speak calmly.

"They said he was dead. They said he'd had his head blown off. But it was lies."

Diantha was held speechless by the suffocating horror that arose in her. She couldn't tear her eyes from the bundle the woman was carrying.

"He's not dead," she screamed. "He didn't have his head blown off. He didn't, *he didn't*!"

She staggered away, clutching the bundle, the very thought of which made Diantha feel sick.

"Come along," Cranning said, taking her arm.

"Did you see what she was holding—?"

"No, my lady, and neither did you," Cranning said firmly. "It was probably just some old clothes."

"Yes," she gasped, "old clothes."

The road seemed endless. Now the moon was high in the sky, throwing the scenes below into livid relief. They trudged on, one mile, then two, while her mind whirled around, wondering what she would find when she reached her destination.

"Look, my lady!"

Cranning was pointing at a cart that had lurched

into a ditch and stopped there, still with the horse between the shafts. She looked around. There were few people on this stretch of road, and those there seemed preoccupied.

"Quick!" Cranning dashed to the horse and began to unharness it. "Can you ride bareback?" he asked in a low voice.

"I'll try."

"It can't be much further."

"Hey!"

They'd been seen. In a moment three disheveled soldiers appeared out of nowhere and converged on them.

"Now, here's rich," one of them said with a leer. "A horse, and some amusement."

He reached out to Diantha. She felt his hand against her face. Revulsion blotted out everything else. She pointed the gun wildly and pulled the trigger. The man screamed as her bullet went into his leg. The next moment Cranning had done the same to one of the others before being felled by a blow from the third.

The man came at Diantha. She could feel the hot stink on his breath as she pulled the trigger again. The man fell back, clutching his shoulder and swearing.

"Cranning!" she cried.

"I'm all right, my lady! Get going now, quickly!"

He helped her up and slapped the horse's rump. At first it was hard to keep her seat without a saddle, and with every bone in her body aching, but she soon found the knack. She'd already done so much tonight that she'd never dreamed of before, that this was nothing.

She knew now that she was getting close to the battlefield. Men were trailing away from it, supporting each other tiredly. Mostly they walked with their heads down, but sometimes one would raise his head, and Diantha saw that their eyes were stunned, their faces ghastly. They were like men who'd glimpsed hell and would never be the same again.

An ominous quiet seemed to be everywhere, and the terrible words *All dead!* rang in her ears. They weren't all dead, but those who lived were like walking corpses.

"Please . . ." She stopped two men who were staggering alone together. "Can you tell me—?"

One of them raised his head. A dirty bandage was around his brow, and blood streaked his face. "Boney's defeated. The Prussians came in time," he said in a hoarse whisper. "The French are in retreat."

"Thank God!" she said fervently. "We won!"

"Yes, we won," he whispered. "We won, we—" Hoarse sobs convulsed him. "We won—we won—" He half collapsed, retching and sobbing against his companion, who drew him away.

She understood then. Even the victory was terrible.

At last she reached the battlefield. All was desolate. The moonlight touched swords, turning them to silver. Men lay with sightless eyes turned up to the sky. Now and then the sound of a horse neighing dolefully echoed across the field.

Diantha looked out over the dreadful scene. The land fell away into a valley, and at the far side she could see it rise again, strewn with dead and dying men. People moved from corpse to corpse. Some were like herself, seeking a loved one. But others would be looters, ready to kill if they were approached. She crouched down and began to move quietly, searching dead faces, praying frantically not to find the one she sought.

She saw a man lying on his face a little apart from the others. He didn't seem to be wearing a military uniform, and her heart lurched painfully. She cried her husband's name, throwing herself down beside him, and pulling him over into her arms.

But it was a stranger. Perhaps somewhere a woman like herself was praying for him to return safely, but her prayers would not be answered.

She rose, her body shaking with sobs. There was so much death about her, and suddenly it seemed impossible that Rex could be alive. She wanted to tell him that she loved him, that she was to bear his child. He had a right to know these things, but it was too late. Her pride and blindness had sent him away in ignorance, and it would pursue her forever.

She stumbled on, calling his name through her tears. The wilderness stretched around her, fading to vast horizons from which there was no escape, condemning her to spend the rest of her life uselessly repeating the words of love that he would never hear.

No one could survive in this charnel house without going a little mad. She knew her reason was deserting her when she heard her own name called. It floated toward her from thin air and she looked around, bewildered, wondering why Rex was calling her when he was dead.

"Diantha!" The sound came again. It seemed to be all around her, but then her head cleared enough for her to hear that it was coming from one direction. A man was calling her in a voice full of love and fear.

"Diantha!"

She whirled and saw him.

"Rex!" She began to run toward him, stumbling,

sobbing with joy and relief. He held out his arms to her and she ran into them, feeling them close about her like steel bands, keeping her eternally safe.

"Darling, what are you doing here?" he asked huskily, between kisses.

"I came to find you. Oh, Rex, Rex—I love you—hold me—hold me forever."

He tightened his arms even more, content to kiss her and ask no questions.

"I love you," she said again, when she could speak. "I've been such a fool. I've loved you from the start, but I was afraid to recognize it. Oh, Rex, tell me it's not too late."

"It could never be too late, until the last moment of my life," he told her.

They clung together in silence. Explanations could wait. They had found each other at last, and that was all that mattered.

"I came to find you," she whispered. "George is all right. They brought him back on a cart, and he's at home. The doctor says it isn't serious."

"Thank God!"

"I was afraid for you, searching here. You might have been killed. Bertie's at home, too, with a slight wound. And Anthony Hendrick was there. I sent for Lady Bartlett. Rex, she told me everything, about my father and how he died. You should have told me. It can't hurt me now."

"I wasn't sure how you'd feel. You seemed to idealize him. It's haunted me since the day we married, made me feel as though I was deceiving you. When she turned up in Brussels I was appalled. All my worse nightmares had come true. I had to do what she wanted, but it was from fear, nothing more. What I felt for her once was a boy's self-delusion, and it was over long ago."

"She told me how she blackmailed you into helping her. I've been so wretched, thinking that you still loved her."

"I love no one but you," he said fervently. "And I never will."

"You love me," she murmured.

"Do you despise me for it very much?" he asked with a hint of a smile.

"Oh, Rex, I was such a fool. I didn't understand anything about love. I thought I didn't want you to love me, but I do—*I do*—"

He kissed her fiercely, and she returned his embrace with her whole heart. There, surrounded by death and destruction, they discovered their love, and the start of a new life.

"I married you under false pretenses," he confessed. "I fell in love with you that first evening, but how could I say so when you warned me away from ever speaking of love? I couldn't tell you how I felt in case you refused me. I thought once we were married I could teach you not to fear love. But you seemed to go out of your way to torment me, first risking your life on Nestor, then capturing the heart of every man in sight and flaunting your triumphs. I died a thousand deaths from jealousy. I told myself they meant nothing to you—"

"It was true. I think I was trying to make you jealous, but I was too ignorant to know myself. I never cared for any man but you, but you seemed so indifferent."

"Indifferent? Whenever you waltzed with another man I wanted to knock him down and carry you off in my arms. I stayed away from you as much as I could, so as not to see you play off your tricks. I was so afraid to give myself away and win your scorn by begging you to love me."

"Let's go home now," she begged. "Back to Brussels, and then back to England as soon as we can. I want our child to be born there."

"Our child?" he echoed in delight. "Diantha—"

"I should have told you before, but I was so afraid I'd lost you forever."

"You'll never lose me," he vowed. "This is our beginning. You're right, my beloved. Let us go home."